PONY FOR KEEPS

Other Books by William Corbin

GOLDEN MARE

HIGH ROAD HOME

DEADLINE

PONY

FOR KEEPS

by WILLIAM CORBIN

Illustrated by Peter Burchard

Coward-McCann, Inc.
New York

PONY FOR KEEPS

1

HE came into the world sometime between midnight and dawn on a sweet-smelling morning in June. He had four tiny hoofs with a little white sock for each and a white blaze that ran from his wisp of a forelock down to his velvety nose.

The first human creature in all the world to see him was Katty Lou, who shouldn't have been there at all. And it was Katty Lou who named him.

Kneeling there in the dew-damp grass of old Evan March's pasture, she hugged herself tight to keep from blowing up into a million pieces with the excitement and wonder of it. The sun was just barely squinting over Mount Hood's snowy shoulder fifty miles away, lighting up the sky while the fir-clad hills to the west remained in shadow. Standing above Katty Lou, Pepper shifted her dainty feet nervously and stretched her muzzle down to lick the silken head. She had foaled many times before, but still it was always new. Besides, she wasn't really sure that a breathless little girl with an old coat over her pajamas was an altogether safe sort of creature to have around at a time like this.

Without thinking about it, as though reading the mind of a Shetland mare were the easiest thing in the world, Katty Lou spoke softly, almost in a whisper. "Don't you worry, Pepper. I wouldn't hurt him for a billion dollars. He's beautiful. He's the most beautiful thing there is."

Whether Pepper was reassured or not there was no way of knowing. At any rate she didn't offer to drive Katty Lou away with kicks and bites as many mares would have done. Instead she quietly got on with the job assigned to her by the mysterious forces of life. And because she did so, Katty Lou was witness to a sight she knew she would never forget if she lived to be as old as Oregon itself.

The foal was lying with his legs tucked under him — legs no bigger around than Katty Lou's wrist. Pepper left off licking him and nudged him gently with her nose. He lifted his head and stared around with eyes as soft and wondering as a fawn's.

His head bobbed and lolled comically, uncertainly supported by a neck that hadn't yet found out what it was for.

In a moment Pepper nudged him again, this time from behind, and with a heaving motion he untucked his forelegs and thrust them out in front of him. Katty Lou's dark eyes grew wide, for now she knew. Pepper was telling him to stand up.

Another nudge, another heave, and the tiny pony thrust at the ground with his forefeet and shoved himself into a sitting position. Again Pepper nudged at his rump. He gathered his hindlegs under him and heaved again while Katty Lou held her breath. He was almost on his feet when one leg gave way and down he went with a little grunt. Katty Lou's breath went out of her in a gasp, as though it were she who had fallen. She wanted to jump up and help him, but something told her Pepper wouldn't like it. She had to content herself with watching, straining every muscle in her own small body, while the process began all over again.

More nudging, hunching, heaving, and then suddenly — like the miracle of a flower opening its petals — a brand-new creature stood upon the earth, his tiny legs spread wide. He staggered, he

swayed, his head rolled around as though it were fastened on with rubber bands, but he stayed on his feet, and Katty Lou found herself laughing with triumph and joy. Before she could think she cried, "Why, he's all tipsy!"

She laughed again as he struggled to keep his treacherous legs beneath him where they belonged, but at the same time she felt terribly sorry for him. Walking seemed an impossible thing to ask of so new a creature.

Suddenly then, a horse neighed shrilly from somewhere near the March barn, beyond the pasture and the tree-lined creek to the west, and Katty Lou's delight was shattered. The neigh reminded

her of where she was, and the thought of where she was reminded her of Mrs. Kirby.

Katty Lou had been living with Mr. and Mrs. Kirby for nearly three weeks now. Mrs. Kirby was short, stocky and quick-moving. She was pleasant enough, on the whole, but she had a way of speaking which made it plain to everyone that her opinion on any subject was the only opinion worth having. As far as Katty Lou could tell, there was almost nothing she didn't have an opinion about. It was always a strong one and she expressed it in a flood of words. Mrs. Kirby could say more words in five minutes, Katty Lou decided, than she herself had said in her whole life.

On the very first day, Mrs. Kirby had made a little speech — for her a very short one — in which she said, among other things, "Now we want you to be happy with us, Katherine Louisa, and you're free to do anything you like, within reason. There are the Bayliss girls down the road to play with — very nice girls. And the Newtons, just beyond. They have swings and all sorts of things to play on, although I must say Frank Newton — they call him Fig — could find better ways to spend his money — what little he's got of it — than on all that kind of foolishness when his poor wife has got nothing to do her washing in but a machine that must have been made before the Civil War. But the only place I don't want you to go — and I must insist on this — is across the road. That's the March place. They're all big rough-talking men, and it's no place for a little girl. One of them — the youngest one — even got arrested once. You'll see girls over there, and boys too, but I can't imagine what their parents are thinking of, exposing them to such influences. The place is absolutely *alive* with horses, and I've never known any good to come of fooling around with horses. I know a thing or two, believe me, about these horsy crowds. All the gambling and drinking and carrying on — you wouldn't believe it. I know all about it because years ago — this was back in Montana — my youngest brother — Harold, his name is — got in with a crowd like that and, well, it just about ruined him. Spent all his money — what he didn't gamble away — on fancy saddles and things, and finally got it so bad his wife — poor thing — couldn't stand it any longer and she left him. Best thing that could have happened, as it turned out, because it brought him to his senses and they've got three children now and Harold has a fine job down in Los Angeles in an aircraft factory. And will he even go *near* a horse any more? You bet your boots he won't. So you'll be a good girl and not go over there, won't you, Katherine Louisa?"

Katty Lou, feeling slightly dizzy, had swallowed and said, "Yes, ma'am." There wasn't, after all, anything else she could have said.

Remembering this conversation now, Katty Lou suddenly felt the old familiar fear shrink and shrivel her and she darted quick glances all around, like a frightened fawn seeking cover. In spite of her promise, here she was at the March place, and it wasn't the first time either. It was the worst, though, because this time she wasn't in the hiding place near the barn; she was out in the middle of a pasture where anyone could see her — not only Mrs. Kirby but the March men too, and she didn't know which would be worse. It had taken almost more courage than she could command to slip out of bed before real daylight, out of the house, across the road and around to the pasture, and now her courage was suddenly all used up. She took one last, yearning look at the foal, who was nuzzling eagerly now at his mother's flank. In a moment he would be having the first meal of his life. Then, holding up her pajama legs, Katty Lou whirled and ran down the sloping pasture toward the road, her bare feet twinkling in the sunlight just beginning to touch the grass.

Not until she reached the safety of her tiny room under the eaves of the shabby old farmhouse was she free — at least for a while — from the fear that had been a part of her for as long as she could remember.

Back beneath the worn old patchwork quilt, she lay staring for a long time at the jagged crack in the windowshade as the rising sun turned it into a thread of gold. She wasn't seeing the crack at all; she was seeing four tiny, glistening black hoofs as they took their first steps, the delicate white-booted legs that were much too long for the little body, the innocent, soft, uncomprehending eyes. Without knowing it Katty Lou hugged herself as if she were holding the colt's silky-soft neck in her arms.

It was as happy a time as she had ever known, but at last it ended with the sound of Mr. Kirby's waking-up cough and the slap of his bare feet as he dressed. It was the beginning of another day.

2

THE fear that always shone from the big dark eyes of Katherine Louisa Denton was as much a part of her as her glistening black hair, her quick birdlike way of moving, her small-boned body that was really strong for a girl of eleven but which managed to seem delicate all the same. The fear was like the air around her. It was simply there, and she seldom thought about it.

It was a fear of people mostly — any people — and when she did think about it, about how it began, and when, she could remember only a thing that had happened long ago when she was little. It was her earliest memory.

She had been living with a Mrs. Cadwallader. There must have been a Mr. Cadwallader too, but he was gone from Katty Lou's memory. She remembered Mrs. Cadwallader only because of the name and because of the big lump on one side of her nose. And, of course, because of what she had said.

Katty Lou had asked why her name wasn't Cadwallader too, and Mrs. Cadwallader said, "Because we're not your real parents. We're your foster parents, dee-er." She always said "dear" as if it were two words, and she said it a lot.

"Then where are my real parents?" Katty Lou had asked. "Are they — are they dead?"

"Not that I know of, dee-er."

"Then why don't I live with them?"

Mrs. Cadwallader sighed impatiently. "I suppose, dee-er," she said, "it's because they don't want you."

That was all there was of the conversation, and the memory. The rest of it had gone on inside Katty Lou's head. Not all at once, but over the weeks and months and years. It wasn't reasoning, really, it wasn't anything she could put into words; but what it amounted to was the belief — growing always stronger — that if her parents didn't want her then there must be something wrong with her, something terribly wrong. She didn't know what it was. She spent many agonizing minutes in front of mirrors, studying herself, and decided she was ugly. Her eyes were too big, her face too small, her hair too thick and black. But there was something else too, because she knew other ugly children whose parents seemed to want them. She couldn't find out what it was and she was afraid to ask, but she was convinced that whatever it was it must be quite clear to everyone else. People had only to look at her, talk to her, and they would know at once. Especially other children. She knew this when she went to school for the first time, and school became a torture. Knowing that the other children would immediately know the strange and horrible thing that was wrong with her, she sat silent and wooden-faced in her classes, never looking at the others or speaking unless there was no way out of it.

Because she acted that way the other children thought there really was something wrong with her, and the cruel teasing began. When they grew tired of teasing, they simply left her alone, which was exactly what she wanted. The story was the same in every new school she went to, and already there had been five of them — five new schools and five new sets of foster parents who were paid by the county to take care of her. None of them could make head or tail of a little girl who almost never spoke unless spoken to and who always contrived to be out of sight when strangers came around.

The Kirbys were the latest. Miss O'Connor had driven Katty Lou to her new home in the familiar black Chevrolet with the county seal painted on its side along with the words WELFARE DEPARTMENT in gold and blue lettering. Miss O'Connor was the one who came every other Saturday to visit Katty Lou and ask about how she was getting along.

Miss O'Connor, it seemed to Katty Lou, came closer than anyone had ever come to being what might be called a friend — a real, living friend, that is. Her other friends were imaginary — like Marie Madeleine DuBois and Winifred Smythe-Wingate, with whom she carried on long whispered conversations when she was alone. Often she spoke to them about "my friend, Miss O'Connor" and always Marie Madeleine or Winifred had something nice to say in reply, such as "Wasn't that a lovely dress she wore today," or "I wish my hair was yellow and wavy like hers. It's absolutely beautiful."

13

The strange thing about Miss O'Connor was that she was the only person — aside from Marie Madeleine and the others, of course — who seemed to be blind to the thing that was wrong with Katty Lou. Other grownups pretended not to know, but Katty Lou always knew they were pretending. With Miss O'Connor it was different. She really *didn't* know. Katty Lou could tell by the way her soft blue eyes lighted up each time she came, as if seeing Katty Lou was a new and wonderful thing, and the way her red lips turned up in a smile as bright as raindrops in the sun.

Even in the beginning Katty Lou had wanted very much to talk to Miss O'Connor, and lately, if they were together long enough, she found that she could — almost as easily as she talked to Marie Madeleine.

During the fifteen-mile ride to the Kirby place Katty Lou had been silent at first, as usual, while Miss O'Connor talked in the voice Katty Lou always thought of as bubbly. She had told about the Kirbys. Mr. Kirby worked in Portland as a shipping clerk, whatever that was, and ran the small farm on which they lived. They were fine people. The country would be a wonderful place to live.

Katty Lou must try really hard this time to make friends with people. Katty Lou listened carefully, not because she was much interested in the Kirbys but mostly because she liked to hear Miss O'Connor talk.

It wasn't until Miss O'Connor said something about the neighbors across the road that Katty Lou pricked up her ears. "The people there," Miss O'Connor was saying, "raise horses and Shetland ponies. They train them and show them in all the big horse shows. They train horses for other people too, and give riding lessons. Oh yes, and they have a drill team, children about your age driving ponies in cute little carts. It's quite famous and appears in horse shows too. Maybe" — here Miss O'Connor gave Katty Lou the kind of look that always made her feel as if they were sharing a secret — "maybe you could get to be one of the drivers some day!"

Before Katty Lou could stop herself she looked up with a glow in her eyes. "Oh, I'd like that!" But before the last word was out she knew she never could do it — not with all those people around, especially the boys and girls. She was excited all the same. The thought of just being close to horses and ponies was enough to make the idea of another foster home bright instead of dreary.

Never in her life had Katty Lou met face to face a member of the horse family, large or small, but she thought she must have read a thousand books about them. To her they were the most beautiful creatures in the world, and the nicest — much nicer than people.

Her wonderful horsy thoughts broke off as Miss O'Connor laughed. "As a matter of fact, I used to go to school with one of the March men. Gather up your things now. We're almost there."

After the introductions were over Katty Lou settled herself in the little room that was to be hers — her good dress and good pair of shoes in the closet, her extra pair of jeans in the battered old dresser. While she was still a little numb from her first barrage of words from Mrs. Kirby, Mr. Kirby invited her — rather timidly, it seemed — to "have a look around the place."

He was a small, bony man with a wisp of gray hair that stuck up from the crown of his head, making him look like a middle-aged kewpie doll. Katty Lou was relieved to find that he left most of the talking to his wife — probably because he didn't have any choice. On their tour of the little farm he only pointed things out, telling what they were in as few words as possible.

Directly behind the house was a small white building. He pointed at it and said, "Pump house." Then led the way down a path to a large building painted red which had weathered a comfortable brown. "Chicken house," Mr. Kirby said, which didn't seem really necessary, since the squawking, muttering and complaining Katty Lou heard couldn't have come from anything but chickens. He took her inside where, partitioned by chicken wire from the large space for the hens, was a small room filled with sacks of feed, egg baskets, and on a table two or three crates of eggs ready for market. There was also an ancient iron stove beside which stood — or rather sat, because it didn't seem in good enough health to stand — an old rocking chair. Mr. Kirby noticed Katty Lou looking at it and made, rather apologetically, his longest speech yet. "I come out here to smoke my pipe. Mrs. Kirby can't stand the smell of it." Katty Lou didn't quite know why, but she liked him better because of it.

Outside again, Mr. Kirby pointed to a small

gray building. Through its open doors she could see the front end of a small tractor. "Tool shed," he said.

"Oh," said Katty Lou, hoping she sounded interested.

Mr. Kirby indicated a small, velvety-green pasture in which a lone red cow was grazing. "That's Betsy." Katty Lou thought it a very dull name, though of course she didn't say so. She would have named the cow Gloriana, or perhaps Gwendolyn.

Then he pointed to where row upon row of small, neat trees stood, each in its circle of shadow. "Filberts," he said, then added in a burst of talkativeness, "Six acres of 'em."

As he and Katty Lou walked back to the house she could tell that he was working up courage to say something. She could tell because it was a thing she was always having to do herself. At the back steps he achieved it. "I hope," he said, stopping to clear his throat, "I hope you'll — uh — like it here."

Then it was Katty Lou's turn to work up courage and she said in a very small voice, looking down at her shoes, "Oh, I know I will."

At the first opportunity she slipped away to have

a look at the place across the road. Standing behind the laurel hedge which was just low enough to look over, she could see a good deal but not nearly enough. She could see straight up the lane to the rambling one-story white house about a hundred yards from the road. At the entrance to the lane was a post bearing a sign with the name MARCH in big red and white letters. Above the name was painted a horse's head, also in red and white. Behind the house was a huge white barn, with the same horse's head outlined in red under the peak of the roof. There was a scattering of other smaller buildings, all white, and a white rail fence ran around the whole place.

Among the buildings Katty Lou could see several cars. People and horses were moving about and she could hear their voices faintly, but it was all too far away to be seen clearly. If there were only some way she could get closer — to see without being seen. . . .

With a guilty start she caught herself. Her promise to her new foster mother was hardly an hour old, and already her mind was busy with ways of breaking it. She turned resolutely away from the March place.

Many times in the next few days Katty Lou would suddenly hear the high, exciting neigh of a horse, perhaps an answering nicker from another, and there would be the pounding of hoofs on hard turf, sometimes a man's voice raised in a sharp command. It was almost too much to bear and her traitorous thoughts would sidle off and sneakily busy themselves with the problem of how to find a way to go and look at the horses and their riders. Only *look* at them — that was all. . . .

Sometimes, to get her mind off the whole thing, she would go out in the little pasture and talk to Betsy. It didn't help much. Betsy was all right, as cows went, but she was a poor substitute for a horse.

The first week was nearly over when something happened that was to change everything and set Katty Lou's feet on the path of wrongdoing.

She came downstairs that morning to find Mrs. Kirby busily piling an assortment of things into a grocery carton. There were bed sheets, towels, a hot water bottle, a few kitchen utensils and other things. Mrs. Kirby turned animatedly to Katty Lou. "I'm afraid I'll have to leave you alone a part of every day for a while, dear," she said. "We heard shocking news last night." She seemed more happy than otherwise about the shocking news. "Our good neighbor, Mrs. Armishaw, had a stroke, poor dear. She's going to need constant attention, and of course poor Mr. Armishaw can't do it. He has to be away at his job, and he can't afford to hire nurses at those awful prices. So Mrs. Bayliss and I are going to divide up the day. I'll do for her in the mornings and see that she has her lunch. Then Mrs. Bayliss will take over early in the afternoons and . . . "

She rattled on cheerfully while Katty Lou ate her oatmeal and toast. She said Katty Lou could help too, by doing some of the chores she herself would be doing if she were here. A few minutes later Mrs. Kirby had picked up her carton and was gone.

That was the beginning of the temptation.

Quick at everything she did, Katty Lou couldn't make her household tasks last longer than an hour or so. The long morning crept by with the siren song of horsy noises from across the road growing more insistent every moment. It was worse the second day, and on the third she began her life of deceit.

It began in small ways, as all such lives do. She merely went for a little walk, a perfectly innocent thing to do. If she happened to wander somewhere near a horse, it would only be an accident, with no harm in it.

What she found that day and the next was that a little creek formed the eastern boundary of Mr. Kirby's filbert orchard. The same creek ran through the March place, making the boundary line between two fields. From the road it curved around and back, reaching a point about forty feet from the rear end of the barn. A heavy growth of small trees and brush along the creek provided perfect concealment. Between the barn and a high corral made of smooth poles was a small, dense thicket of dogwood, laurel and sword fern from which almost everything that went on could be seen. The only point in the whole route at which there was danger of being seen was the forty-foot dash from the creek to the thicket.

It took Katty Lou two days of calling herself harsh names before she summoned the courage to make the dash. She chose the noon hour, assuming that everyone would be inside having lunch.

Everyone was — with one exception which nearly led to her undoing.

Crouching by the creek, heart pounding, she took a deep breath — she would have closed her eyes too if she could have done without them — and ran. Seconds later she was flat on her stomach, burrowing through the ferns. When her heart had regained its normal beat, she parted the ferns and looked out, and her eyes grew even wider than usual. At the side of one of the buildings, not twenty feet away, stood two horses, their tails switching lazily at flies. They were saddled and a stirrup was hooked over the saddle horn of each. Katty Lou was proud to know from the books she'd read that this was a warning to anyone who might want to ride that the cinch had been loosened for the animal's comfort and must be tightened before the horse could be ridden.

While she feasted her eyes on their beauty, a ghost of a breeze brought to her nose the sharp, exciting, unmistakable smell of horse. They were Arabians, she was almost sure, judging from the high arched necks and the narrow, in-curving noses. Not until later did she find out she was only half right. The horses were the Marches' favorite combination, a Morgan-Arabian cross. One was a creamy palomino, the other as black as Katty Lou's hair.

While she watched, her eyes taking in every beautiful line, she began rather absent-mindedly eating the leftover meatloaf sandwich she had brought along in a sack. That was the mistake she made. To her the smell of horses was intoxicating, but there are those who like the smell of meatloaf better. Katty Lou's revery was suddenly and frighteningly broken by a rustling in the ferns behind her. She whirled, stared, and froze. She was looking straight into the face of a huge black-and-silver German shepherd.

For what seemed an hour his alert, intelligent eyes bored into hers. Then his mouth came open in a doggy smile, about a yard of pink tongue appeared, and his tail began to move in majestic arcs from side to side. His eyes moved to the sandwich. Weak with relief, Katty Lou laughed softly, broke the sandwich in two and gave him half. He held it in his mouth a moment, swallowed once, smiled again, and looked at the other half. She hesitated, smiling back at him, then thrust it toward him. "You can have it," she said, "if you promise you won't eat *me*."

When the second half of the sandwich was gone he regarded her with kingly solemnity for a mo-

ment and then moved closer. All at once the big tongue came out and licked her face from chin to ear. Then he sat down beside her. Her arm slid around the massive shoulders and she pressed her cheek against his.

The first friend had come into her new life.

3

AFTER that Katty Lou came every day to the hiding place in the thicket, always remembering to bring a snack for Shadow — for that, she soon learned, was the big dog's name. Each day he would sit with her for a while before going off on business of his own.

During the all-too-short hours she spent there her eyes and ears were busy every minute, and soon she felt she knew the three March men as well as she had ever known anyone. There were no March women.

From a second peephole among the ferns, Katty Lou could see into the big corral where the Marches worked by turns at the job of breaking two-year-olds to the saddle. There was old Evan March himself — tall, gray and scraggly, with skin the color of an old saddle, a high, humped nose and a voice Katty Lou thought of as "gritty but nice."

It was a voice he used freely enough most times, she noticed, but when he worked a green horse he did it in utter silence. At those times, she could see, he let his hands do his talking for him, and his craggy face became masklike in his absorption with the job. Only his crinkly, darting gray eyes betrayed the fire within him, undimmed by his sixty-odd years.

To Katty Lou those were some of the best times of all — when old Evan jackknifed himself into the corral between two poles and strode along in his high boots, deliberately, purposefully, with a hackamore dangling from his bony hand, straight up to whatever horse to be schooled was dancing nervously inside, saddled and expecting the worst.

What followed was a kind of music, and Katty

Lou could listen to it hours later when she was in her bed and the house was dark — the countless little leathery creaks that are made by a horse, a saddle and man in motion, the soft thud of hoofs on the bare and dusty ground, the hoarse, hard breathing of the sweating two-year-old.

Then there was Cal, the older son. He was even taller and broader than his father, but he looked very much like him, with the same humped nose, the same lively eyes, the huge, powerful hands. But his way of working the horses was quite different. He talked to them all the time, his big voice booming out an unending barrage of words, about half of them words that a little girl shouldn't be hearing. At first Katty Lou had been startled, shocked and a little frightened, but after a while she understood that he meant nothing by the words and in time she could listen without even hearing them.

Homer, the younger son, was both like and unlike the others. He worked as hard, laughed as often and as easily as they did, and gave the same impression of strength, but he was of a slimmer build than they were and moved with a kind of grace they didn't share. His nose was straight, his eyes blue not gray, and Katty Lou thought he was much handsomer than the others. She decided he must look like his mother.

Another thing she liked about Homer was his way of saying funny things with a perfectly serious face. All three men were always making jokes and laughing, but to her Homer seemed the funniest.

There was the morning she arrived at the hiding place to find Cal, in a dirty blacksmith's apron, trimming the hoofs of Fancy Man, a big bay gelding. Although the sun was bright it didn't seem very hot to Katty Lou, but Cal's face glistened with sweat and the muscles of his big arms bunched and rolled with the strain of his work. Fancy Man, who didn't in the least appreciate what was being done for him, was being as uncooperative as possible. Double-roped to iron rings on either side of the doorway, he couldn't get away, but he could still maneuver with his rear end. The usual uncomplimentary profanity was rumbling out of Cal's throat in a steady stream. Tied nearby was Gay Girl, who looked almost like a twin to Fancy Man. They were three-year-olds whose schooling was now complete and they had been sold, Katty Lou learned, as a pair. Homer was to deliver them in Hillsboro, forty miles away.

Coming around the corner of the barn, Homer grinned mischieveously as he heard his brother's monologue and saw him strain to wrench Fancy Man's big reluctant hind hoof into the proper position between his knees. Then Homer leaned against the door frame with exaggerated ease and inspected his fingers with the air of a woman examining a manicure. "Oh dear," he said, "that reminds me — I've *got* to cut my fingernails."

Cal grunted without looking up. His big steel clippers were quickly and efficiently cutting away a half-moon of hoof paring. "I'll cut 'em for you, sonny," he said grimly. "Right up to the elbow."

Homer sighed. "No sense of humor. You trim Gay Girl's already?"

Glancing up digustedly, Cal said, " 'Course not. She keeps 'em gnawed off that way herself."

Homer addressed Fancy Man. "What are you waiting for?" he said. "This is your last chance to kick his head off." Whistling, he crossed the barnyard to the long, compartmented equipment shed, backed out the pickup truck, hitched it to a red and white horse trailer and drove it into a position to load the two horses.

Fifteen minutes later he was sweating as hard as Cal had been and it was Cal's turn to stand idly by, making helpful suggestions. Gay Girl, it seemed, had decided opinions about horse trailers — all of them negative. Time after time Homer backed her off, calmed her down, then led her firmly forward, only to have her balk the minute her feet touched the loading ramp, or veer off to one side or the other.

From the hiding place Katty Lou silently cheered each new attempt and suppressed an inward groan at each failure.

Even the lure of a can of oats which Homer rattled enticingly in front of the mare failed to weaken her determination to have nothing to do with the trailer. Katty Lou knew there were other ways to make her go in, but they called for the efforts of two men and she knew Homer couldn't bring himself to ask for help.

The older man was squatting on his heels with Fancy Man's lead rope under his arm, watching with an attitude of childlike fascination. "Tell you what," he said brightly. "Why don't you jack her up and back the trailer under her?" Later he said, "Guess you'll just have to ride her over there. Let's see, it's about eleven now — you ought to make it before dark."

After another five minutes of fruitless struggle, Homer paused, wiped his streaming brow and grinned ruefully. "Okay, I give up," he said. "Go get a rope, will you?"

Cal remained in his squatting position. "What'll you bet I can't load her by myself the first try?"

Homer answered promptly. "I'll bet my new saddle against your old one."

"It's a bet." Cal stood up, led Fancy Man into the trailer, tied him, then came back and took Gay Girl's rope from his brother's hand. Grinning wickedly, he said, "I'm going to hate myself for this." With that he marched forward, up the ramp and into the trailer, with Gay Girl right behind, meek as a puppy on a leash.

At first both Homer and the unseen Katty Lou stared unbelievingly. Then she saw the dawn of understanding on Homer's face and a minute later the truth burst upon her. Of course! Gay Girl wouldn't load unless Fancy Man was already in the trailer. Cal must have known that and Homer didn't. Katty Lou was thinking how mean it was of him to take advantage of his brother when the big man, coming down the ramp, chuckled suddenly. "Keep your saddle," he said. "I don't bet on a sure thing."

Another thing Katty Lou liked especially about Homer was his way with horses. All the March men were firm and gentle, but Homer was the most gentle of all. He talked to them too, but much more softly than Cal, and only to praise or reprimand. He would say "Easy, little gal, easy! Prancing's pretty, but it's bad manners." Or, "That's a good little guy! You'll be winning ribbons like your daddy one of these days." Katty Lou loved to watch all three men, but Homer was her favorite. Part of this feeling, perhaps, came from the fact that he was in charge of the pony drill. She had seen the drill the first time from across the road because it took place before she had discovered the hiding place.

Early that afternoon a number of cars began to turn into the March lane, bringing boys and girls. A little later a dozen ponies appeared in single file from behind the house, each drawing a little white cart driven by a boy or girl. Striding after them came a tall figure in a bright red shirt and a broad-brimmed white hat — the man Katty Lou learned later was Homer March.

In the field to the left of the house they formed a line, each pony facing Homer, who stood for a while, talking to them. Then came the sound of a whistle and the drivers began putting the ponies through a series of complicated maneuvers. They wheeled to the right, then to the left as a single group. In groups of two, four and six, they performed figure-eights and other patterns, coming to a halt at last side by side in a single line.

Katty Lou watched breathlessly from behind the laurel hedge. It was a beautiful sight — the ponies going at a fast trot, their little hoofs moving almost too fast for the eye to follow, the shiny spokes of the cartwheels twinkling in the sunlight. She could hear Homer's shouted commands — "Pick it up, Tiny, pick it up! You're dawdling! You, Star, let her out! Quick, Nugget, close up that gap! Get back in line, Baldy — you're edging out!" It was a while before Katty Lou realized he was addressing each driver by his pony's name.

With a hopeless, aching desperation Katty Lou

longed to be one of those children, to hold the reins in her hands, to fly effortlessly along behind one of those dainty, high-spirited creatures, to be one of a group instead of forever alone, to be free of her burden of fear.

When she did begin to go to the hiding place in the thicket she carried with her a heavy load of guilt. It was her nature to be obedient, but the March place drew her to itself as a whirlpool draws a floating chip. She could no more stay away from it than a boy can stay away from a window when a parade is going by.

She saw the ponies again soon after she found the hiding place. Unfortunately she couldn't see the drill practice from there because the house and barn were in the way, but it was almost as good to lie there watching as the girls and boys led their ponies out of the barn, backed them between the cart shafts and harnessed up.

Homer was everywhere, seeing that things were done right and lending a hand to the younger ones when they needed it. He handled Tiny himself because the little stallion was dancing frantically, snorting, neighing shrilly and misbehaving in every way he could think of. "What's the matter with him?" asked the boy who was to drive him. Homer laughed and pointed to Tony, a big black gelding hitched to a post nearby. "The little devil wants to get at Tony. He hates big horses — outside of the mares, that is. Wants to kill 'em."

"But gee," the boy said, "Tony'd knock him for a loop with one kick."

Homer shook his head emphatically. "Don't let his size fool you. A Shetland stallion is a fighting fool. This little fiend broke loose one time and tangled with a Morgan stallion we had. Darn near ruined the Morgan before we could drive him off with ax handles and anything else we could lay our hands on."

"Wow!" exclaimed the boy, looking at Tiny with new respect.

"Don't ever forget," Homer said. "When you're driving this rascal you've got a package of TNT at the end of your reins."

Katty Lou saw the ponies harnessed for drill two more times the next week. The second time was the day before she first saw Pepper's newborn colt.

The children were leading the ponies out when one of them, a girl about ten years old who wore her yellow hair in braids, ran up to Homer, who was making emergency repairs on a bridle. "Pepper's not in the barn, Homer!" she said worriedly.

He slapped his leg in annoyance. "Doggone it, Sue," he said, "I forgot to tell you. You didn't need to come today because Pepper won't be working."

"Oh," Sue said. Katty Lou could see the disappointment in her face. So, evidently, could Homer, for he looked at Sue unhappily, then brightened. "Tell you what. I'll get Janet to trade off with you — let you drive Dreamy part of the time."

Watching Sue's grateful smile, Katty Lou wondered for another of many times what this man who was so kind and gentle with horses and children could possibly have done that was so bad he had to be arrested. She couldn't make herself believe it, and yet she knew Mrs. Kirby wouldn't have told a falsehood.

Sue turned to go, then whirled back, looking worried. "What's the matter with Pepper? Is she sick?"

Homer smiled down at her. "No, I'm just giving her a little vacation. She's about to foal."

"Oh!" Sue exclaimed. "Where is she?"

Homer pointed. "I put her over in the east pasture, by herself." He added regretfully, "I guess you'd better not go see her. They get a little nervous just before it happens."

The girl was wide-eyed now, and so — though she didn't know it — was Katty Lou. "You mean," Sue said, "she's going to foal just any time now?"

"Wouldn't surprise me a bit," Homer said, "if there was a brand-new bit of horseflesh on the place by morning."

Long after Katty Lou should have been asleep that night she lay awake, alternately in a fever of excitement and a chill of dread at the daring of what she was going to do. But there never was any question that she would do it. Something said that she, Katty Lou Denton, had to be the first person in the world to see Pepper's foal, and that was that.

4

KATTY Lou's daring expedition to see the newborn colt provided quite enough excitement for
one day. It gave her plenty to think about, and to
talk about to Winifred and Marie Madeleine for a
long time. She couldn't know, of course, that there
was still more excitement to come — but of a very
different kind.

Before Mrs. Kirby left for her nursing duties
that morning she led Katty Lou to the vegetable
garden beside the chicken house and pointd to the
sprawling pea vines, brilliantly green in the morning sun. "The first two rows should be picked today," she said. "They're the earliest. If you'd pick
and shell them so I can get them ready for the
freezer tonight, I'd be very grateful."

"Yes ma'am," Katty Lou said. "I will."

Mrs. Kirby had a nice way of assigning chores,
which made Katty Lou even more willing than

usual to do them. Ordinarily she would even have welcomed the pea-picking job, but this wasn't an ordinary morning. Already her mind was busy with schemes for going to see the colt again and she was eager to get started.

Her fingers fairly flew from vine to vine, but the picking seemed to take forever. Her back began to ache from stooping and her legs from squatting, but she refused to stop long enough to rest them. The shelling went even slower and it was mid-morning before the huge yellow bowl was heaped with peas on the kitchen table and four buckets of empty pods stood on the floor. Katty Lou managed to carry all four buckets at once to the chicken house and scatter the pods on the floor for the swarming hens. Then she quickly made two sandwiches, one for herself and one for Shadow, and started for the creek.

She was clinging fast to the hope that Pepper might have come down to the creek to drink and had stayed nearby, so that Katty Lou could be close to her and the colt without having to venture into the open where she could easily be seen from the road or the house. At the point where the creek began to bend toward the barn a sharp "OH!" of disappointment escaped from her mouth. Pepper was grazing far up the slope of the pasture and the colt lay near her. At that distance he was nothing but a shapeless, motionless little lump.

Katty Lou sat in the grass by the creek's edge for a long time, hoping they would come nearer, or at least that the colt would get up so she could see him. When nothing happened she tried to convince herself that no one would see her if she crossed the open pasture, but she knew all the time it was too great a chance to take. At last she gave up and made her way as usual to the hiding place.

Old Evan was sitting on the corral fence giving a lesson to a woman who was obviously a beginner and even more obviously nervous. Katty Lou had to smile as she listened to Evan's reassuring monologue. "Easy does it, ma'am," he was saying. "Just walk her gentle. . . . Loosen up a little on them reins. . . . Thaaat's right, thaaat's right. . . . No ma'am, that little ol' horse is gentle as a kitten. You could lay right back on that horse an' have you a snooze. . . . Just point your toes out a little there, You hug her too tight an' she thinks you wanta go somewheres. Thaaat's the stuff. . . ."

Katty Lou had seen the horse in action before. It was a buckskin mare named Ginger with a reputation for being hardmouthed and difficult to handle. She could tell by the sweat that matted Ginger's coat why she was behaving so well now. Before the woman arrived Evan himself had mounted and put into the mare what he always called "the fear o' God an' womankind," which consisted of making her do everything she didn't want to do — not once but half a dozen times. By the time an inexperienced rider climbed onto her, Evan's mere presence was enough to keep her in line. And now he was making the speech about how safe and gentle Ginger was. Katty Lou laughed silently. Evan's cheerful falsehood made her think of the queer man the Marches called Orvie who had come a day or two before to shoe several horses. Orvie, she had gathered, was the most accomplished liar in the whole Northwest.

She had been in the hiding place when an ancient and incredibly dirty car came rattling and snorting into the barnyard and wheezed to a a stop. Hitched to it was a small trailer which slumped dejectedly to one side because of a broken spring. In the trailer was a jumble of tools and a sheet of iron blackened by countless fires. Out of the car stepped — or rather rolled — one of the oddest figures Katty Lou had ever seen. Her impression was of stubby legs, immense shoulders, long, powerful arms covered with curly gray hair, and a dirty-whiskery face from which small, bright eyes peeped out in a strangely monkeylike way.

Cal, who had stepped into the barn a moment before, came out with a saddle slung over his shoulder. Catching sight of the queer-looking man, he grinned broadly. "Well, Orvie, you're late. What held you up — another long-distance chat with the White House, or what?"

The little monkey eyes looked up at Cal for a long time. Then, in a high, squeaky voice that nearly made Katty Lou giggle, Orvie said, "Well, as a matter of fack, the gol-durndest thing happened. You wouldn' believe it."

"Why, Orvie!" put in Cal, sounding a little hurt. "Of *course* I'd believe it."

"Well," Orvie continued, draping a massive elbow over the car's open door, "'bout a hour, hour'n a half ago, I was on my way over here. I'd just gone past the old Grange hall over to Snake Hollow when —"

"Hold it, Orvie," Cal interrupted. Easing the saddle to the ground, he called over his shoulder, "Hey, Sonny! Orvie's about to tell why he was late. Come on out and listen so he won't have to tell it again!"

In a moment Homer appeared in the barn door, wearing a grin as broad as his brother's had been. "Go to it, Orvie," he said. "I'm all ears."

"Gol-durndest thing," Orvie repeated. "I was comin' along by the Grange hall over to Snake Hollow when all of a sudden a young gal come a-bustin' outa the brush 'longside the road, wavin' her arms an' yellin' at me. Purty gal — purtiest I ever seen — found out later she was one a them movin' pitcher stars. Anyhow, I stopped, natch-er'ly, an' she come a-runnin' up an' says, 'Oh, help me, help me! They're after me!' So I says. . . ."

The story went on for a good ten minutes, growing more and more bloodcurdling. It ended with Orvie turning over to the police the three kidnapers from whom the girl had escaped and whom Orvie had disarmed and overpowered single-handed.

When the story was over, Katty Lou saw Homer

wink at Cal. "By golly," he said, "I can hardly wait to read all about it in the papers. You'll be a hero, Orvie!"

Orvie shook his head. "Taint gonna be in the papers. The gal, she figgered the publicity'd be bad fer her career, so she got the p'lice to promise they wouldn' say nothin' about it. An' I promised I wouldn't never tell her name."

Cal, looking grim with the effort of keeping his face straight, said, "Anyway, I'll bet you're due for a mighty handsome reward."

"Already got it," Orvie said placidly. "She set right down an' wrote me a check fer five thousan' dollars."

Homer tried to whistle his amazement but didn't make much noise because he too was having trouble with his face. "May I look at it, Orvie?" he asked. "I never saw a check for that kind of money."

Orvie shook his head regretfully. "Wish I c'd show it to you, but I plunked it right inta the bank."

Homer looked at his watch thoughtfully. "I didn't know the bank was open that early."

47

Hesitating for only a moment, Orvie said, "The p'lice, they got the bank president t'come down an' open up special."

Cal made a choking noise which he managed to turn into a series of coughs, while Homer whipped out a handkerchief and hid behind it, blowing his nose loudly.

"Well," said Orvie, apparently realizing the ice was getting a little thin, "best I git to work. Where's them horses you want shod?"

Thinking about Orvie now, Katty Lou decided that his elaborate brand of falsehood made Evan's handy little lie about Ginger's trustworthiness seem like unvarnished truth.

She moved to her other peephole and saw Cal at work loading a small truck with hay from the barn. He was tossing the heavy bales as easily as if they had been made of cork, his huge hands swallowing the handles of the hay hooks. Homer was nowhere to be seen.

She was just turning back to watch Evan again when Shadow appeared. He came from the barn and at first she didn't see him. Then suddenly she heard his noisy panting and looked around to see the big face with the grin on it thrust through the peephole toward the barnyard. She grinned back at him as she reached for his sandwich, not giving a thought to the fact that the rest of him, including his majestically waving tail, must be outside the thicket, plainly visible to anyone who happened to look.

"I'm late, Shadow," she whispered. "But it really wasn't my fault. You see —"

She got no farther because all at once she heard Homer's voice, dangerously close, and mildly puzzled. "Hey, old boy, what've you got in there — a kitten?" Shadow backed abruptly out and Katty Lou tried desperately to make herself as small as a kitten, if not smaller. The bushes rustled, stirred, and suddenly she was looking straight into the face of Homer March.

For one of the longest moments she had ever known, he stared down at her. She had never seen him this close before, and what struck her at first, along with the brilliance of his blue eyes, was his size. Because his brother and father were bigger she had thought of him as just about ordinary size, but up close he looked every bit as big as one of

49

the horses. While she crouched there, frozen, his wide mouth widened even farther in the warm smile she had already come to know so well. "Well, by gosh —" he said softly, "another wood nymph! I thought we'd cleaned 'em all out when we burned the brush a year ago. Come on out, nymph, and we'll see what you look like standing up." He stepped back, still smiling, and held out his hand invitingly.

Katty Lou's eyes followed his as if invisible wires were pulling them. For a horrible moment she felt as though she were being torn in two. Half of her wanted desperately to get up, to walk out into the sunlight, to speak to the big smiling man, to be like other girls. But the other half, the half where the dark fear dwelt, cringed back in unreasoning terror, screaming at her to get away as fast as she could go.

Her eyes must have betrayed the tug-of-war behind them because Homer March spoke again, even more softly than before. "Won't you come out? I sure would like it."

He meant it — he really meant it, she told herself fiercely. It was true! For an instant — the merest eye-wink of time — she felt as if she were going to do it, but then another voice spoke. "Who you talking to, sonny — the birds and bees?"

Katty Lou flashed a startled glance at Cal, who was standing on the truck looking curiously toward his brother, still holding a bale of hay between the hooks. A moment later, almost in a single movement, Katty Lou had gathered her feet under her, whirled and was dashing across the open space toward the haven of the creek.

For a while Homer March stood staring at the place where she had been. His smile was replaced by a puzzled frown, as he bent and parted the dogwood branches with his hands. Then he called over his shoulder, "Cal, look here a minute."

The two men squatted on their heels, peering into the shadowy thicket. Pointing, Homer said, "See how these ferns are flattened out — here, and over there? And look at that — sandwiches! She's been coming often, and staying a long time. Now I wonder —"

"Who is she?" Cal wanted to know.

"Don't know," Homer said. After a moment he added musingly, "Pretty little thing. But scared — good Lord, Cal, you should have seen those eyes of hers!"

Cal grinned lopsidedly at his brother. "Can't say I blame her — looking at that thing you use for a face."

Homer shook his head impatiently and got to his feet. Cal stood up too. "I can't get over those eyes," Homer said wonderingly. He seemed to be talking mainly to himself. "There's somthing wrong. Nobody ought to be that scared — 'specially a little kid."

"What could she be scared of?" Cal asked.

"I don't know," Homer said. "People, maybe. But I aim to find out."

"Uh-oh!" Cal said. "Here we go again — another stray!"

"What are you talking about?"

"You know what I'm talkin' about," the big man said. "All my life, and half of Dad's, we've had some broken-down critter under foot because of you. Mangy kittens that weren't worth drownin' — baby birds that didn't have enough sense not to fall out of a nest and had to have worms dug for 'em — even a by-gosh *rat* that got his leg busted in a trap. And then the time Dad had to shoot a horse — I thought we'd have to rope you to a gatepost, and —"

"What's all that got to do with anything" Homer

interrupted. "All I said was I aimed to find out what —"

It was Cal's turn to interrupt. "Don't fire up your boilers," he said, slapping his brother's shoulder affectionately, a wallop that would have buckled the knees of a smaller man. "Whatever you do's all right with me. You know that."

"Sure," Homer said. "I know it." He seemed a little absent-minded. "But I'm still wondering who she is. Most of the kids for miles around have been here one time or another and —"

"Say!" Cal broke in. "Come to think of it, I heard the Kirbys across the way were taking another county kid. I bet —"

"That's it!" Homer said. "I should have thought of it myself. And being a county kid would account for the way she is. Must have had a rough time, by the look of her. Poor kid."

"Yeah — poor kid," echoed Cal. He heaved a mighty sigh and squinted at the sun. "Well, this isn't getting my hay loaded."

As Cal strode back to the truck Homer stood a moment longer, thinking. Fortunately for his peace of mind he had no way of knowing what Katty Lou was doing.

She was lying face down on her bed, a handful

of the old patchwork quilt clutched in each small, strong hand. She was crying bitterly and without a sound. She didn't want to cry, she hadn't expected to cry, and she didn't even know why she did it, but she was doing it anyway.

She was crying because of many, many things — things even Katty Lou didn't know about, or knew about only in a vague, frightening way, the way a person knows almost but not quite where the furniture is in the dark. They were things like loneliness and fear and the lack of something to love or be loved by. Then there was shame, like a bitter taste deep in the throat. She had run like a frightened rabbit from the smiling man who held out his hand to her, the man who wanted — *really* wanted — her to come to him, the man the other children ran to eagerly, their faces plainly showing what he meant to them.

Then came the worst thing of all — the knowledge that now, having done this foolish, shameful, fear-driven thing, she could never go back again because she couldn't bear to face him. It would have been better, she told herself over and over as the silent sobs tore at her chest one after another, if she had never gone there in the first place. It would have been better if she had never known anything about the beauty and mystery and wonder of a tiny newborn pony. It would have been best of all if such a person as she had never been born at all.

Luckily there is something about the machinery of misery which tends to reverse itself after it has gone as far as it can go. And it did with Katty Lou. When she had reached the very depths of her unhappiness, the point at which it seemed certain that nothing worse could ever happen to her than had already happened, an idea came to her. It was an idea that contained at least a grain of hope, and she began the long climb back from the bottomless hole of despair.

The idea took shape gradually and soon she was sitting up on the bed, scrubbing at the tearstains with her hendkerchief and feeling just a little foolish. The idea was simply this: pride and shame wouldn't permit her to go back to the hiding place, where she was sure to be seen again, but there was still a chance that she could be near the colt and perhaps make friends with him. The Marches wouldn't even know about it.

After a while she said, aloud but very softly,

"Marie Madeleine, do you ever cry? The wet, messy kind of crying, I mean?" And Marie Madeleine said quickly, "Oh, I do it all the time. I'm really an awful baby, I guess. I wish I could be like you, Katherine Louisa. You almost never cry."

Katty Lou felt a good deal better. Good enough, at any rate, to go down and straighten up the house for Mrs. Kirby.

5

THE next morning Katty Lou started for the creek as soon as Mrs. Kirby had gone. She left her chores for later, knowing it wasn't the right thing to do, but she couldn't bear to wait.

It was a beautiful morning. The sky was bluer than blue really ought to be, the way it is in picture postcards. The grass of the pasture was greener than green. As she walked along, staying close to the protection of the creek's brush, a gray-digger darted out of the brush just ahead, saw her, whirled with a flirt of its tail and darted in again. She laughed and called out to the place where it had vanished. "If you only knew it, silly, I wouldn't hurt you for anything." Mr. Kirby didn't like graydiggers because they stole nuts from the orchard, but it seemed to Katty Lou as though there ought to be enough nuts for Mr. Kirby and the graydiggers too.

As soon as the words were out of her mouth she came to a sudden halt, feeling strangely uncomfortable. She was hearing her own words over again, only this time they were being said by Homer March — to her. "If you only knew it, silly, I wouldn't hurt you for anything!" That must have been the way she looked to him — like a gray-digger scampering off through the brush, fleeing from dangers that didn't even exist.

She went on, thinking about this new idea, until she reached the bend in the creek. After that there was room for nothing in her mind but a sudden, unbelieving delight. There, by the very edge of the creek, stood Pepper with her baby at her side.

Seeing Katty Lou at the same moment, Pepper jerked her head up from the grass and turned to face what could be a danger to her foal. Katty Lou stood still as a tree and called out softly, "Don't be scared, Pepper. It's only me. Remember?" The colt too turned his delicate little head toward her with soft, curious eyes. He was too young to know the meaning of fear.

In a moment Pepper decided there was nothing to worry about and went back to her grazing. Not

58

until then did Katty Lou notice a strange thing. A long chain led from Pepper's halter to an iron stake in the ground. Someone had staked her there, and at once Katty Lou knew who the someone was. But why had he done it? The pasture was fenced. Pepper didn't need to be tied. Instinctively Katty Lou knew the answer and a quivering kind of excitement filled her as she began moving slowly toward the ponies. Homer March had known she would come.

As she drew near, her eyes caressing the babyish head with the little tuft of hair between the ears — the tuft that would some day become a forelock — Pepper looked up again worriedly, and moved around the colt, placing herself between him and the intruder. Katty Lou smiled approvingly. "That's right, Pepper, don't take any chances," she said. She decided to sit down, to watch and wait. Sooner or later Pepper would get used to her being there and she would be able to ease her hands of the itch to stroke and pet the velvety head and the funny little body.

She chose a spot where a leafy sapling overhung the edge of the pasture along the creek and was heading toward it when the second surprise of the morning caught her eye. A breath of breeze came by and a white thing fluttered briefly among the foliage in front of her, about on a level with her eyes. Coming nearer, she saw that it was a sheet of paper stuck on a twig, and something was written on it.

She approached it warily, as if it might conceal a trap, and then she saw the pencil — a stub of a pencil hanging from the same twig by a string. Her glance darted around, probing the shadowy brush, but there was no one to be seen. She reached out her hand, pulled it back quickly and looked around again. A moment later the paper was in her hand and she was reading the words, printed with a heavy hand.

Dear Nymph: The little beggar needs a name. Can you help me out? Below were the initials H.M.

For a moment — she didn't know why — Katty Lou felt as if she were going to disgrace herself with tears for the second time in as many days, but the feeling went away and left in its place a bubbling warmth. Quickly, before she could lose her nerve, she seized the pencil and dropped to one knee, using the other for a desk.

Below Homer March's initials she printed in

capital letters a single word: TIPSY. Then she replaced the paper and pencil and sat down, a little surprised by her own bravery.

As though her sitting down were a signal he had been waiting for, the tiny pony with the brand-new name suddenly did a thing that drove from her mind all thoughts of the note, the man who had written it, of everything but Tipsy himself.

He had been standing quietly beside Pepper, his much-too-long legs widespread. Without warning he flung up his little head and whirled, throwing his hindquarters into the air, coming down stiff-legged. Then he was off at a fast trot which quickly turned into a canter. He looked like a child's rocking horse, and Katty Lou, who had jumped to her feet without knowing it, laughed with delight.

About fifty feet away he wheeled and stopped, looking back at his mother with a comical questioning air, as if asking why she didn't come and play too. Pepper, watching him anxiously, obviously would have gone to him if she could. But she had learned long ago by painful experience — as he too would learn some day — what happens to a pony who tries to run while chained. Instead she did a nervous little dance, as though she were standing on something hot, and called out to him to come back.

Tipsy was a disobedient child, even at the age of one day. Whirling, he bounced up and down once or twice, as if he were on springs, and ran off again. Pepper danced more frantically, called to him again, and even pulled at her chain on the chance it might possibly be loose. But it wasn't.

Katty Lou was worried too. What if he should run to the far side of the pasture and into the electric wire that surrounded it? What she didn't know yet was that no colt will lose sight of its mother willingly. Sure enough, he wheeled again and stopped to see if Pepper was coming. This time she must have seemed a vast distance away and he must have felt suddenly alone in a huge and motherless world. He leaped into a dead run and came charging toward her, his tiny feet drumming softly on the turf. Like a boy first learning to drive a car, he wasn't as good a judge of speed and distance as he thought he was and he failed to slow down quickly enough. He banged into Pepper's side with a soft little grunt and then stood breathing heavily and looked a little foolish. Katty Lou laughed aloud again and Tipsy turned his head and stared at her curiously. He had yet to learn that people are strange creatures who are forever making peculiar noises with their mouths. A few of those noises, he would some day learn, had meaning for a pony. Most of the few would mean that he was supposed to do something he didn't much want to do, but by far the greatest number of those noises meant nothing at all. People were simply noisy animals, like chickens.

Watching Tipsy's antics, Katty Lou had been seeing — though she didn't think of it that way — another of the mysterious forces of life. He had been born, he had got to his feet as quickly as possible, because from the dawn of time every horse creature had needed to be able to run for its life almost from the moment of birth. Now, like the children of all the higher animals, including man, he was learning to play.

He didn't know, of course, that play had a purpose laid out for him a thousand thousand generations before he was born. That purpose was to make him use the brain and nerves and muscles that had been given him so that those muscles and nerves and that brain would be strengthened, quickened and sharpened with only one end in view. Some day they might save him from the enemies who would kill him and eat him if they could. So he played, knowing only that he felt full to bursting with life and couldn't stand still.

Katty Lou didn't think of these things any more than Tipsy did. She only watched and told herself over and over again that anything so beautiful and small and full of life should be held and protected from all bad things forever. Katty Lou, in her own way, was playing too. She was playing at having, some day, a small human creature to love and care for.

6

IN Katty Lou's life it had always been true that good things — what few there had been — came sooner or later to an end, and she should have been on her guard now.

The next day began like the one before, without a cloud in the sky and without a hint that disaster lay ahead. As a matter of fact, it very nearly turned out to be the finest day of all.

This time she did her work first so she wouldn't have to keep it on her mind during her visit to Tipsy and Pepper. She made the beds, washed the breakfast dishes, and then went to work in the garden thinning out the rows of young turnips, carrots and beets, as she had been told. Finishing at about ten, she took the beet thinnings to the kitchen, washed them carefully, wrapped them in paper towels and put them in the refrigerator, ready to be boiled for supper. She put her sandwich in a paper sack, then filled the sack with the tiny carrots she had pulled. With them she hoped to bribe Pepper to let her get closer to Tipsy. Not for weeks, of course, would Tipsy be interested in green things. His neck would have to grow and catch up with the length of his legs before he could reach the grass. Even then for a while he would have to spread his legs awkwardly to get his head down far enough.

Reaching the pasture Katty Lou noticed once more that Homer March had been there before her. Pepper's stake had been moved a short distance farther along the creek where the grass was untouched. Tipsy was having a nap, lying flat on his side. As Katty Lou approached, he raised his head, gave her a sleepy look, then put it down again. She went up to Pepper, walking slowly, talking all the way and holding out a handful of the carrots.

It worked. A few minutes later Pepper was chewing placidly at the little pile of carrots on the ground and Katty Lou was sinking cautiously to her knees beside the colt. The fuzzy little neck was even softer to her touch than she had imagined. His head, when she stroked the little white blaze, was much harder. Somehow she had expected him to be soft all over.

His response at first was a soft little snort, but soon he struggled to his feet and stood looking at her inquiringly. Though she was still on her knees

her head was higher than his. Then, while she stayed quite still, he slowly stretched his neck toward her. The little nose, no bigger than a baby's fist, came nearer. She could feel the warmth of his breath. His velvety lips touched her cheek and nuzzled it experimentally. She almost laughed, because it tickled, but she didn't for fear of frightening him. Apparently satisfied that she smelled all right and felt all right to the touch — though of course she didn't smell and feel as good as his mother — he turned, trotted over to Pepper and helped himself to a snack.

The snack made him feel good and he played a while, running in circles with his stubby little tail held high like a flag, flinging his head around, bouncing, bucking and doing his imitation of a rocking horse. Katty Lou watched in a happy trance, her eyes following every movement until at last he tired himself out and came trotting back, to the obvious relief of Pepper. who had stopped eating to watch him anxiously.

It was then that a voice spoke behind Katty Lou. "Hi-ya, nymph."

She jumped to her feet, whirling at the same moment, to find the blue eyes of Homer March smiling down at her. He added quickly, "Please don't run off. I brought something for the little guy and you might like to see it."

Again Katty Lou felt the dreadful torn-in-two feeling. She wanted to run, yet she wanted even more to stay. If she stayed it would mean that as sure as bad luck this man would find out about the awful thing that made her different from other girls. He would be the polite kind who pretended not to know it, but he would know it all the same. For reasons she couldn't understand it mattered terribly that Homer March, of all people in the world, should not know.

These thoughts scurried frantically through her mind like frightened mice during the second in which she stared at the big man with wide and startled eyes. Then another thought flashed by — a saving thought that gave her the extra thimbleful of courage she so badly needed. Might there possibly be a chance that Homer March was a person like Miss O'Connor? Could he maybe — please, God — be blind to the thing that was wrong with Katty Lou Denton? While the thought was still new and strong she opened her mouth and in a voice so small she could scarcely hear it herself she said, "What did you bring?"

By the way Homer March let his breath out slowly and carefully she knew he had been holding it quite a while. "This," he said, holding up a big hand from which dangled a tiny halter made

70

of reddish, hand-stitched leather. "What every well-dressed pony colt should wear," he added. "Come on, let's how he looks in it."

He started toward Pepper and Tipsy without a glance at Katty Lou, as if he hadn't a doubt in the world that she wouldn't run away, and somewhat to her surprise, she didn't. Even more to her surprise she was hardly frightened at all.

He gave Pepper a friendly slap on the rump and rubbed Tipsy's little topknot with his knuckles, bending almost double to reach him. "Tipsy, my lad," he said — and a little thrill rippled all through Katty Lou's body to know that the name she had given the pony was really to be his — "I brought you a present you don't particularly want."

He kneeled, slid a big arm around Tipsy's shoulders and lifted the tiny forefeet off the ground. With his other hand he suddenly held the halter out to Katty Lou. "Here, you slip it over his head while I hold him. He isn't going to take to the idea right off." He was careful not to look directly at her as he spoke.

She was just as careful not to look at him as her hand closed over the smooth, pliant leather. His voice went on steadily, reassuringly. Though she didn't know it, he was treating her as he would have treated a frightened, half-wild filly. "The part you've got your hand on there," he said, "goes over his ears. That's it — that's it. Now just bring the snap up to the ring — Say, you're way ahead of me! All right now, little fella, go on and try to shake it off." He let Tipsy go and stood up. Katty Lou stood beside him, watching.

At first Tipsy did nothing but stand there looking up at them. Then he seemed to realize that this strange, bothersome thing on his head wasn't going to go away. His little ears went back, saying in plain horse language that he wasn't at all pleased. He gave his head a tentative shake. The thing didn't go away. He shook it harder. Still the thing didn't go away. This, he seemed to think, was a serious matter calling for drastic measures. Suddenly he lowered his head and whirled completely around, evidently hoping the thing would stay where it was. It didn't. Next he tried to run away from it. That didn't work. One by one he tried all his tricks, with a lot of head shaking thrown in for good measure.

In the middle of it all Homer March slapped his thighs and his voice boomed out with laughter.

A moment later Katty Lou realized with a start that she was laughing too and she made herself stop abruptly, darting a glance at Homer to see if he had noticed. But his eyes were still on Tipsy and his teeth gleamed white against the brown of his face as he laughed. He was still chuckling when he said, "That little rascal's got gumption. Most of 'em give up quicker." Almost as soon as he said it Tipsy came trotting back to Pepper. He gave his head one last regretful shake and then stood quite still. Homer knuckled the little topknot again. When he spoke he didn't seem to be talking to anybody in particular. "We'll give him a while to get used to it and then we'll start halter-breaking him."

"How do you do that?" The words were out before Katty Lou had time to think. She felt herself turning a disgusting telltale red. But apparently Homer didn't notice. He spoke as easily as if the two of them were already in the middle of a long conversation. "Nothing to it," he said. "Just snap a lead rope onto that ring and let him pull till he finds out it isn't getting him anywhere. After that you lead him around, turn him, stop him, start him, and all that. Make him get it through his head he's got to go when you pull on that rope. Same way with a big horse. You outpull him when he's little and all his life he'll think a man, or a little girl, is stronger than he is — even when he's ten times the weight of the man and thirty times the weight of the girl." He paused a moment, then snapped his fingers. "Say! I bet you could take over that little chore for me — that is, if you'd want to." He spoke as though the idea had just occurred to him.

Want to! Katty Lou could think of nothing in the world she could have wanted more — unless it was to be like other girls. She could almost feel the rope in her hands now, with Tipsy tugging at it, see him stopping when she said "Ho," starting when she clicked her tongue. But she couldn't bring herself to say the needed words. She had courage enough only to look up into the big man's face and then quickly away.

What she didn't know was that her eyes had spoken for her. "Tell you what," Homer said, as though everything had been settled. "In the morning when I come to move Pepper's stake I'll bring a lead rope and you can get to work any time you take a notion."

74

He turned to go, then hesitated and turned back. She had the impression that he was feeling almost as shy as she was. "Might be handy," he said, "if I knew your name."

It wasn't too hard for her to say "Katherine Louisa Denton," but it was very hard indeed to add, staring hard at the ground, "It's Katty Lou for short."

"Katty Lou," he repeated thoughtfully. "I like it." He paused, apparently trying to decide whether or not to say what was on his mind. She didn't know which she wanted more urgently — for him to go or to stay. At last, gesturing toward the barn, he said, "Thought you might like to know — if you go back up there in those bushes, nobody'll bother you." Then he was gone, his long legs in their faded jeans taking him quickly around the bend of the creek.

For a long time Katty Lou's eyes stayed fixed on the point at which he had disappeared. Then she looked down at Tipsy, who had lain down for another nap, his forelegs tucked neatly under him. "You don't know how lucky you are to have him for your master," she said softly but fervently. "You just don't *know*."

75

When the position of the sun warned her it was time to go home, she had made tremendous progress. Pepper was beginning to accept her as a normal part of the scheme of things, While Tipsy had forgotten there ever was a time when there weren't two she-creatures around to cater to his wishes. Several times he had come to her for the express purpose of having his head scratchd. She knew that was the reason because when she didn't scratch it he nudged her impatiently with his nose. He allowed her to pet him all she wanted —or anyway nearly all. He even paid attention now and then to what she had to say.

In her absorption with the colt she very nearly stayed too long, and as things turned out she might as well have.

Waking suddenly to the realization that Pepper's puddle of shadow on the grass was bulging ominously toward northeast, she gave Tipsy a final hug and a hasty goodbye and ran for home. Five minutes later she was hastily cleaning up the crumbs from her sandwich-making when Mrs. Kirby arrived, carrying a sackful of soiled linen.

She said "Hello, dear," and set the sack on the drainboard. Katty Lou hurried to take the soiled things to the washing machine. "My goodness, isn't it hot!" Mrs. Kirby went on. "I declare, it makes me think about the heat wave we had one time back in Montana when I was, oh, thirteen or fourteen. I can remember it just as well as if it —" Katty Lou was never to hear about the heat wave in Montana. Mrs. Kirby broke off abruptly and a slight frown came over her square, solid face. Then she moved closer to Katty Lou and sniffed. "Horses!" she said explosively, and Katty Lou went rigid in a kind of paralysis. "Horses!" repeated Mrs. Kirby. "Katherine Louisa, can you explain how you happen to have the smell of horses on you?"

Fortunately for Katty Lou, who couldn't possibly have said anything in reply, Mrs. Kirby didn't give her a chance to. "Well, I'll just bet *I* can explain it!" she rushed on. "You've been over at the March place messing around with those horses — though how you could do it after everything I said to you about it I *don't* understand, and I only did it for your own good because it's my duty to see to it that you aren't exposed to the kind of influences my brother Harold . . ."

She went on to tell about her brother Harold all

77

over again, in greater detail than the first time, and by the time she got around to the subject of Katty Lou again she had worked off a lot of her anger. All she said then was, "I'm going to let you off easy this time because maybe I didn't make myself clear when I told you never to go over there. But if it ever happens again — well — that will be another story. Right now I want you to go to your room and spend the rest of the afternoon thinking over what you've done. You may come down at suppertime."

Katty Lou fled gratefully to the sanctuary of her little room. As Mrs. Kirby talked, shame and guilt had grown inside Katty Lou like a huge lump. Even though she knew that Mrs. Kirby's brother and his troubles had nothing in the world to do with the Marches, she still had deliberately disobeyed — and in a sneaky way. Worse than the shame and guilt, though, was the knowledge that the door she had opened with her sneaky disobe- dience — the door to a world that had Tipsy in it, and Homer and Cal and Evan and Shadow, and a host of things her life had never known before — had now slammed shut in her face, and she mustn't open it again. Not ever.

For an endless time she lay motionless and silent on the old quilt, staring at nothing. Cars swished by on the road outside, birds made their busy noises in the big old cherry tree, the chickens chatted in the henhouse. There were two worlds now — a big one where people lived and watched the sun move across the sky, and a tiny one with a crack in the window shade where there was nothing but Katty Lou and shame and misery.

In her little world, time didn't move as it did outside; it sat like a vast and senseless lump, waiting for nothing. It might have sat there forever if there hadn't come to her, sometime during those motionless hours, a thought that brought at least a measure of relief. It wasn't a comfortable thought — just the opposite, in fact — but it set the minutes moving again and brought her up into a sitting position on the bed, her legs tucked under her.

The thought was about Miss O'Connor, who was to come Saturday on one of her regular visits. Katty Lou would tell Miss O'Connor just what she had done and how she had been found out. Just why it should be, she had no idea, but she knew that simply by confessing everything she would feel a little better, that some of the crushing burden of her guilt would be lifted. She longed for Saturday to come.

She was busy thinking just how to phrase the confession when she heard the wheezing of Mr. Kirby's old car and the crunch of its wheels on the graveled driveway. A few minutes later, to her surprise, she heard the sound of his feet on the stairs. He was coming to her room — something he had never done before.

She got up hastily and was smoothing the rumpled quilt when the footsteps stopped outside her door and he cleared his throat apologetically. "Could I — uh — come in?" he asked in his dry voice.

"Yes," she said faintly, and the door opened. "Brought you something," he said, holding out an ice-cream bar wrapped in silver foil. She took it automatically and managed a very small "Thank you."

"Just happened to think of it when I stopped by the store," he added, as if it were something that required an apology. "Go on and eat it, before it gets too soft."

Relieved to have something to do that didn't require conversation, Katty Lou stripped off the wrapping and bit into the chocolate-covered ice cream. While she carefully avoided looking at him, Mr. Kirby shifted his feet, jingled coins in his pockets and cleared his throat twice. In a moment he walked over to the window and stood looking out, as if something fascinating were going on in the cherry tree outside. She felt sorry for him because she knew he wanted to say something and didn't know how to begin. She chewed her bite longer than was really necessary and after swallowing it she was able to say, "This tastes real good."

It gave him the help he needed. "Persons shouldn't take things too much to heart," he said, still staring out the window.

Knowing that he was trying to comfort her brought a tightness to Katty Lou's throat. Even if she could have thought of something to say, she couldn't have said it. In a moment he went on. "We all do wrong things, one time or another. I ought to know, because I've done plenty of 'em myself. But some are wronger than others."

He paused and Katty Lou took another bite of

her ice cream. She felt it was a rather rude and disrespectful thing to do under the circumstances, but it was getting soft and there was no other way to dispose of it. Anyway she was listening carefully. He jingled his coins furiously and went on, still not looking at her. "I'm not much of a hand at saying what I mean, but — well, what I'm getting at is that you didn't do anything so all-fired bad. In your shoes I'd of done worse, by a heck of a sight. It wasn't right, I guess, doing something you were told not to, but —" He shrugged helplessly and turned to face her for the first time. "All I mean is it wasn't a thing you should take so hard and blame yourself for, like it was a crime or something. You're — you're a good girl, and you shouldn't — like I said — you shouldn't take things so much to heart."

He scowled down at his shoes as if they had offended him somehow, and added quickly, "Well, guess I better get out and do a few chores." In a minute the door closed behind him, and Katty Lou stood staring at it with a strange kind of warmth in her chest.

She was still staring at it when the ice cream

slid off its stick and fell to the floor with a tiny plop. She didn't mind losing it at all, and when she set about cleaning it up with her shoe rag she was smiling for the first time in hours.

7

THE next day was Friday — a whole day to get through somehow before Miss O'Connor came on Saturday. Katty Lou got up with the firm resolve to be sensible, to keep herself from thinking about Tipsy and Homer and the horses. More than that, she would get up her courage and go down to play with the Bayliss girls, as Mrs. Kirby was always urging her to do.

While she did her morning chores she kept telling herself just how it would be. She would simply walk down the road, not even glancing across into the pasture where Tipsy was. The Bayliss girls, neither of whom she had ever seen, would be in the yard, on the swings, maybe. She would walk right up to them, pretending she was no different from any other girl, and say, "I'm Katty Lou Denton. Mrs. Kirby said maybe I could play with you."

Then one of the girls would say, "We'd love to have you" and the other would say, "Oh yes! And can you stay for lunch?" They would swing and play games all day. The time would pass and never once would she think of Tipsy.

It was a comforting plan, but even while she planned it she knew in her heart that it would never come about. Never would she have the courage even to go near two strange girls, let alone speak up and offer them her friendship. She found herself taking unnecessary time about each task, then thinking up new ones to put off for a few more minutes the time for starting to the Bayliss place. At last, looking at the kitchen clock, she saw that it was after eleven and decided it would be impolite to go so near to lunchtime. They would feel they *had* to ask her to stay. The decision brought her a vast relief which she pretended didn't exist. She would go in the afternoon, she told herself firmly as she sponged the gleaming top of the kitchen table the second time.

Then, because the urge had been in the back of

her mind all the time, like a mouse in its hole, she went into the living room and, kneeling on the faded green sofa, looked out the window toward the March place.

There, in the field to the left of the house, were three riders. Katty Lou had eyes for only one. His white hat bright in the sun, Homer sat tall in the saddle on his motionless horse with his back toward her. The others, a man and a woman, sat facing him, obviously listening to his instructions.

The mere sight of him brought to Katty Lou's mind the sound of his voice and with it a rush of other sights and sounds, all forbidden now. The most insistent of them, of course, was the sight of Tipsy, the impudent arch of his little neck, the way his stub of a tail stuck out behind him as he ran, the *dollop-dollop* sound of his tiny hoofs, the feel of his hard little head beneath her eager hand, the way she had felt like bursting with love and wonder when he struggled to his feet for the first time in his life.

For a minute it was almost too much for her and she had to look away. She looked down at her hands and saw that they were gripping the back of the old sofa with a desperate tightness. But she couldn't look away for long. The scene across the road drew her like the mysterious force that draws bees back to the hive or birds back to their wintering place. She looked again. The man and woman were trotting their horses now in a wide circle around Homer and, at the moment Katty Lou looked, a strange, disturbing thing happened. He twisted suddenly in the saddle and turned his face directly toward her. Instinctively, for reasons she couldn't possibly have explained, she ducked down below the level of the window sill. An instant later, telling herself disgustedly how silly she was, she straightened up again. At that distance he couldn't possibly have seen a small face in a window covered by curtains except for a little wedge-shaped space at the bottom. But why had he looked? Again she told herself not to be silly. Maybe he had heard a noise, or turned to look at a passing car. Had there been a passing car? She didn't know.

He had turned back now, and by the way his head moved she could tell he was calling out something to his pupils. She went on watching while the man and woman trotted, then cantered, then walked their horses in response to Homer's commands. They were walking when it happened again. This time Homer stood up in the stirrups and twisted around, laying his left hand on the horse's rump to steady himself, and looked in her direction for what must have been several seconds. Katty Lou controlled another foolish impulse to duck out of sight, but for some unexplainable reason her heart began to beat a little faster. She strained her eyes toward him. At that distance his face was only a copper-brown blob beneath the wide white hat, but something — perhaps the way he held his head — gave her the feeling that he was puzzled, even worried. More than that — and here her heart beat faster still — she felt that whatever he was worried about had something to do with her.

For the third time she told herself she was imagining silly, impossible things and went on watching the lesson. By now the Bayliss girls were as far from her thoughts as if they had three heads apiece and lived on a distant planet. Homer's horse — she could see that he was riding Blister today — leaped suddenly from a standstill to a canter in response to one of those invisible signals Homer always used, then slowed to a walk as he came alongside the woman. Reaching across, Homer did something involving the woman's hands and the reins. Probably, Katty Lou thought, he was showing the woman how to keep the reins low and loose instead of high and tight, the way most beginners do, to the bewilderment and discomfort of the horse.

Homer rode back to his place and wheeled his horse around while the pupils started to trot again. Katty Lou was wondering for perhaps the twentieth time how he could make a horse do whatever he wanted it to without moving so much as a muscle, when he turned again and looked toward her with that quizzical set to his head and shoulders. This was once too often to be a mere coincidence, and in spite of telling herself yet again that he was imagining things Katty Lou knew beyond the shadow of a doubt that Homer had gone to look for her at the place where Pepper was staked and was wondering why she hadn't come. The knowledge brought a warmth which dulled, at least a little, the painful ache of remembering things she could never again see and hear and touch. Homer had looked for her and missed her. There was a crumb of comfort in that.

89

She went on watching every move he and the others made, hearing in her mind the music of creaking saddle leather, the plumping of hoofs on the turf, the huffing of the horses' breath. Time, which had passed like a dragging weight before, flashed by and suddenly she knew by Homer's upflung hand — a gesture of dismissal — that the lesson was over and it was noon. He trotted his horse up to the others and the three rode on and disappeared behind the house.

With a mighty, though unconscious, sigh, Katty Lou turned away from the window and climbed listlessly down from the sofa. She was on her feet in the middle of the room when the sudden drum of hoofbeats reached her ear — loud and getting louder. In an instant she had flung herself back onto the sofa and was staring out with eyes that grew wider by the second.

Homer on Blister was pounding down the March lane at a hard gallop, the dust smoking out behind him. Her lungs filled abruptly with air and then refused to let it out. Without slackening his stride the big sorrel took the right-angle turn from lane to road, swept past the front of the house, and in another sharp turn thundered up

the Kirby drive and skidded to a halt at the corner of the house. While Katty Lou still held her breath, unable to move a muscle, Homer swung out of the saddle, dropped the reins to the ground, and strode to the front porch, passing within mere feet of the window.

The sounds of his boots on the loose boards of the porch and of his knuckles on the door, rapping gently, broke her paralysis and she slid to the floor at the end of the sofa, as far from the door as she could get. There she crouched, feeling as if the very beating of her heart might strangle her.

He knocked again, a little harder, and called softly. "Katty Lou!" A shiver ran up her back. He called again. "Katty Lou! Could I talk to you?" Then there was silence, and she thought that surely he must hear the thudding of her heart.

She couldn't answer. She *couldn't*. She couldn't talk to him because he would want to know why she hadn't come to start halter-breaking Tipsy. If she had either to die or to tell him it was because he had been arrested and because the Marches weren't nice people, then she would simply have to die. It was like dying just to think about it.

She heard his step on the porch again and was

able to breathe a little — but not for long. His boots crunched in the gravel along the side of the house and in a few moments he knocked again, this time at the kitchen door. She went rigid all over. That door was open! What if he were to walk right in and find her cowering there like a rabbit in the brush? Her eyes darted wildly around, seeking a place to hide.

He didn't come in. He called her name again and again, and each time the old torn-in-two feeling was like a burning inside her. Then at last he went away.

For a long time after the drumbeat of Blister's hoofs had faded off up the March lane Katty Lou sat on the floor with her arms stretched out on the sofa, her face hidden in her arms. She wasn't crying, because this wasn't that kind of a sadness. It wasn't a sadness at all. It was a terrible, aching feeling of loss. It was as if she had once been full but now was empty, like a desolate old house deserted even by the mice.

She didn't even want to watch the riding lessons from the window any longer. The sight of Homer March would only make things worse.

8

THE next afternoon Miss O'Connor came.

Katty Lou had been watching for the county car all morning, even though she knew it wasn't likely to come until afternoon. At least it was something to do to help pass the endless time and to keep her from thinking about Tipsy, who was so near and yet who might as well have been a thousand miles away, for all the chance she had now of seeing him. Now — or ever.

She was helping Mrs. Kirby with the lunch dishes when she heard the car turn into the drive. She glanced up questioningly. "Run along, dear," Mrs. Kirby said. "I can talk to her later."

Miss O'Connor had just got out of the car, her yellow hair gleaming bright in the afternoon sun. Katty Lou thought, as she had many times before, how nice Miss O'Connor looked. She was taller than many women, though she didn't give the impression of bigness. Katty Lou had decided it must be because she was shaped so nicely and because she moved with a kind of effortless grace. She was smiling now and, in spite of herself, Katty Lou felt a tiny flicker of hope that maybe Miss O'Connor would do something magical that would make things right. The flicker died quickly. Magic wasn't real — and what could she possibly do?

Miss O'Connor bent down and gave Katty Lou's waist a quick squeeze. "Hello, honey," she said. "You're looking fine."

"Hello," Katty Lou said, looking at Miss O'Connor's open-toed shoes, which were small for so tall a young woman.

Miss O'Connor held the car door open invitingly. "Jump in," she said. "We'll take a little drive."

Katty Lou slid obediently under the wheel and over to the other side. The car smelled like Miss O'Connor — a sort of clean smell, like pine needles.

The Chevrolet hummed along the macadam road, the wind whispering conversationally past the open windows. Now, Katty Lou thought. Now is the time to tell her.

Again and again she had rehearsed the words she would use to begin. She had even recited them to Marie Madeleine, who agreed that no better set of words could possibly be used. Now Katty Lou couldn't remember a single one of them. Any minute now, she thought frantically, Miss O'Connor would start talking about something else, and it might be too late. She would lose her nerve.

Then pure desperation spoke, blurting out the words. "Miss O'Connor — I — I did something bad!"

Miss O'Connor's eyes didn't even leave the road ahead. "Not so *very* bad, I'm sure," she said. "Tell me about it." She didn't sound a bit shocked.

"But it *was* bad," Katty Lou insisted with a firmness that took her quite by surprise. "Mrs. Kirby told me not to, at the very beginning. But every day for a long time, I sneaked off anyway and went over to the March place to watch the horses and — and everything."

Miss O'Connor took her eyes from the road long enough to look down at Katty Lou. She was smiling. "So far," she said, "it doesn't sound too awful. Of course you shouldn't have done it if you were told not to. But sometimes temptations get too great — for all of us." She was silent for a moment and Katty Lou could tell she was thinking. Then she said, "What was it you saw that made you want to keep going back, even when you knew it was wrong?"

Katty Lou thought about the question for a long time. She found she was bursting to tell, because until now there had been nobody to share it all with — except Marie Madeleine, of course, but Marie Madeleine and Miss O'Connor were two quite different people. Katty Lou didn't know where to start — there was so much of it. At last she began, a little haltingly, where she might have known she would begin — with Tipsy.

"I saw him the very day he was born," she said, and her eyes stopped seeing what was before them now, envisioning only that magical, never-to-be-forgotten moment. "I was the very first — and I saw him stand up for the first time in his life . . ." She didn't know when the words stopped coming haltingly and began pouring out of her as they had never poured since she was a very little girl. Nor did she know that Miss O'Connor took her eyes from the road from time to time to glance at the glow on the small face beside her, her own eyes soft and full of understanding.

Before Katty Lou broke off, minutes later, shocked by the sudden awareness of what she was doing, she had told Miss O'Connor everything — not only about Tipsy and Pepper but about Shadow and the hiding place and the pony carts, about Homer and Cal and old Evan.

For a long time Miss O'Connor said nothing, and Katty Lou squirmed inwardly, convinced that her outpouring had made her seem babyish and silly. When Miss O'Connor began to talk, her tone showed she had been thinking hard. "Did Mrs. Kirby explain why she didn't want you to go over there?"

"She said," Katty Lou told her hesitantly, "that people who have horses are bad. They gamble their money and — oh — lots of things. It's mainly on account of her brother, only the Marches aren't anything like her brother and all those people. And — and she said Homer had been arrested."

"Arrested!" Miss O'Connor said the word so explosively that Katty Lou was startled. "What on earth for?"

"She — she didn't say."

"I can't believe it!" Miss O'Connor said. "When I knew him in high school he was very nice. Everybody liked him; he was a football star and everything. Of course, people do change when they get older, not always for the better. I heard he was in the war, in Korea, and sometimes war does things to men that —" She stopped, and Katty Lou knew she was thinking a little girl might not understand what she was saying. Katty Lou wished she hadn't stopped, though, because she felt she could understand anything about Homer March — anything at all.

A little later she forgot all about it because Miss O'Connor abruptly applied the brakes and turned in at a farm lane where she stopped and began to back and turn the car around. Stealing a look at her as she maneuvered the car, Katty Lou saw that her lips, ordinarily softly curved, were firm and determined. Fear clouded Katty Lou's eyes. Something had gone wrong. But what was it?

Quickly the fear gave way to a wild, impossible hope. Heading the car back the way it had come, Miss O'Connor said, "Now don't expect a thing from this, honey. You mustn't. But I'm going to have a look at these March people myself. As I told you, I only knew — Homer. Not the others. But if they don't strike me as being as bad as they're painted —" She broke off and added only, "Well, we'll see."

Katty Lou didn't dare look at her. She was wondering if the thing she felt toward Miss O'Connor in that moment was love. She knew what she felt about Tipsy was love. But this was something else. It was like a pain in her chest.

Miss O'Connor stopped the car at the Kirby driveway. "You run on in," she said. "I won't be long."

Katty Lou didn't think to look at the kitchen clock when she went in, but it seemed as if Miss O'Connor was gone forever. Mrs. Kirby's footsteps were moving about in the attic, next to Katty Lou's room. She had said something the other day about cleaning it out. Katty Lou thought guiltily that she ought to go up and help, but even guilt couldn't move her unwilling feet from the front part of the house, where she kept glancing out the window from time to time, hoping to see some sign — *any* sign — of what was going on at the March place. But there was nothing to be seen. Miss O'Connor's car, Miss O'Connor herself, and whoever else was there, were hidden behind the house.

Miss O'Connor had told her not to expect anything, and she tried her very best not to, but it was impossible to keep from imagining that at this very moment Miss O'Connor was talking to Homer and that — well — after anybody talked to Homer everything was bound to be all right.

Keeping her pins-and-needles vigil by the front windows, Katty Lou saw Miss O'Connor's car — hours and hours later, it seemed — the moment it appeared at the head of the March lane. She was waiting beside the driveway when it pulled in and stopped.

Then, in a single, shattering moment, hope vanished as if it had never been. One look at Miss O'Connor's face was enough. That it was a face full of regret and a tender sympathy did nothing to soften the blow. Katty Lou could look at it for only a moment, then had to look at the ground. Through a sort of numbness she heard the car door opened, felt Miss O'Connor's arm circle her waist and draw her gently toward the house, heard her whisper, "I'm sorry, honey. I'm afraid Mrs. Kirby is right. It's no place for a little girl."

Desperately Katty Lou wanted to cry out, to protest, to tell Miss O'Connor she was wrong, that Mrs. Kirby was wrong, that the Marches were good men, all of them, no matter what anybody said. But she didn't know what treacherous thing her voice might do — and anyway she just couldn't. Not Katty Lou Denton. Miss O'Connor's voice went on. "I hoped to find things different — *really* I did."

She meant it — truly meant it. Katty Lou could tell that. But it didn't make any difference. Nothing made any difference now. Now she would never see Tipsy again.

After Miss O'Connor had gone Katty Lou kept asking herself over and over again — uselessly — what could have happened. Had Miss O'Connor heard Cal swearing with particular violence? Had old Evan looked unusually disreputable? Had Homer — ? There she stopped. Not even Katty Lou's lively imagination could picture Homer doing anything that would turn a person against him.

What on earth, then, could have happened?

It was a long time before she found out.

9

NOT until she was much, much older — and possibly not even then — would Katty Lou know whether or not she would have embarked upon a life of deceit if it hadn't been for Mr. Kirby. What she did know was that never in her life would she cease being grateful to the funny, timid little man for starting her — though he didn't know it — on the downward path.

Of course, there was no downward path that Saturday afternoon when Miss O'Connor waved goodbye with troubled eyes and started back to her office in Oregon City, her admonition — for all its gentleness — pressing down on Katty Lou like a weight too great for her strength. "I'm afraid I'll have to tell you you must stay away from the March place altogether. I don't *want* to, honey, because I can tell what that pony means to you.

But I have no choice. Maybe some day you'll understand why."

No, there was no downward path — nor any leading upward either. There was no path at all. There was only blankness, emptiness, and the lost, hopeless feeling of one who has held riches in her hand and had them cruelly snatched away.

In spite of Mr. Kirby's efforts to tell stories about his youth, supper was a strained affair that night. All three of them knew — Mr. Kirby because he had been told in private — the gist of what Miss O'Connor had said to Katty Lou, and all of them did their best to pretend that everything was the same as it had been before. Katty Lou tried valiantly but without much success to hide her desolation. Several times, though, she glanced up to find Mr. Kirby watching her with troubled eyes. When the meal was over and the dishes washed, he wandered into the kitchen in his striped overalls, his old black pipe in his hand, and said with what seemed exaggerated casualness, "Guess I'll take a turn in the orchard. See how the filberts are shaping up. Katherine Louisa, you care to come along?"

Knowing that he was reaching out toward her, trying the best he could to help her, she nodded shyly and followed him out the door, past the barn and chicken house and into the orchard, where late-toiling bees hummed in the leaves of the orderly little trees.

Mr. Kirby plucked the tip of a branch from one of the trees and handed it to Katty Lou. "Feel of it," he said. She did and found the dark green leaves covered with some sticky substance. "Honey dew," Mr. Kirby said. "That's what the bees are after."

They passed a few more trees in silence. Evidently he had forgotten he had come to see how the nuts were shaping up. The cultivated ground was cloddy and hard to walk on and the dust kept sifting in over Katty Lou's shoe tops. She didn't care. Walking in the dust was better than sitting and thinking about what might have been.

Mr. Kirby stopped, fumbled in his overalls and brought out a can of Prince Albert and a matchbox. He made a major operation of filling his pipe and lighting it. Katty Lou waited, snapping dead, brittle twigs off the undersides of filbert branches and dropping them to the ground. She knew Mr. Kirby needed a lot of time to work himself up to saying whatever was on his mind.

At last, watching a cloud of blue-gray smoke drift up and lose itself among the branches, he said haltingly, "Guess there's nothing an old duffer like me can say to make you feel any better — but it's worth a try." He scratched his head with his pipestem before he went on. "I can tell that seein' those horses and all means a lot to you, and — well, doggone it — if you were a boy I'd say it was all right for you to go over there. But for a girl, well, I guess Mrs. Kirby is right. The Marches are a little rough in their ways, though there's no harm in 'em. Bound to be that way, I reckon, in a place where there's no womenfolks around."

He paused, inspected the contents of his pipe critically and pressed the embers down with his thumb. Then he went on. "Like I said before, I don't see any cause for you to feel that going over there was so all-fired bad. By gollies, it doesn't look like much compared to some of the stunts *I* pulled when I was a young sprout . . ."

In a moment he was off on an account of his misdeeds as a boy, saying they were bad but not really thinking so, as Katty Lou had heard grown-ups do before. She was a little disappointed because she had hoped he would go on talking about the Marches, but she tried to give him her full attention, knowing that he was trying to ease her feelings. In spite of herself, though, her mind would wander and busy itself with visions of Tipsy and of Homer March. Each time she would jerk herself back to the present with a feeling of guilt.

It was after one such jerk that she heard him saying, "And then there was the time I took up smoking. My mother was dead set against it. When it came to tobacco smoke, she had a nose like a beagle, and a couple of times she whaled the tar out of me when she smelled it on me. Well, you know what I did — ornery little brat that I was? I got me a cake of real strong-smelling soap and kept it in the pump house. And every time I'd had a smoke with the other boys down by the river or somewhere I'd sneak in there and wash all over — even my head. Then I'd wash my mouth out with that soap!" He chuckled. "Awful-tasting stuff — but it worked. Mother wondered how come I was always so clean, which wasn't natural for me, but she never caught on." He paused, looking back with tolerant affection, as a man will, at the boy whose sins he was condemning in the phrases of adulthood. "Should've had my backside blistered," he said with another chuckle.

There, in that anecdote, lay the seeds of Katty Lou's downfall, though, to her credit, they sprouted slowly and against her better nature.

At the time, she didn't know that seeds of any sort had been planted. It was merely another of Mr. Kirby's reminiscences and she was trying unsuccessfully to think of some way to get him back onto the subject of the Marches.

For a while he said nothing, carefully relighting his pipe, which had gone out. Then, to Katty Lou's delight, he wandered back to the subject himself. "Speaking of tobacco," he said, "I even took up chewing once. That was in the trenches, in France, back in 'eighteen. Lot of the boys did it then, because we weren't allowed to strike a light after dark. Evan March was one of them. Only difference is that he never gave it up and I did."

"Oh," said Katty Lou, startled into speech by the answering of her unspoken wish, "were you in the war together?"

Mr. Kirby shook his head. "I didn't know him then. We were in different outfits. But I soon heard about him. That boy came near to winning more medals than anybody else in the division."

Katty Lou stared wide-eyed, picturing old Evan as a young man doing heroic deeds. She was glad when Mr. Kirby went on. "Fighters every one, those Marches. Likely you didn't know there was an older son. He died in the next war — on one of those Pacific islands."

"Oh-h-h!" said Katty Lou, not knowing she had made a sound.

"And the next son," Mr. Kirby went on, "the one they call Cal, carries scars the like of which not even a doctor would like to see, on account of falling on a Kraut grenade to save the lives of his buddies. . . . And the young one — he was over there in Korea, and there are those who say the only reason he came out alive was that there wasn't a bullet made that could fetch him down." Suddenly Mr. Kirby sighed deeply, as though his talk of war and death had brought up things he didn't like to remember. "Guess I'm shooting off my mouth too much, girl."

In the silence that followed, Katty Lou became

aware of things that were going on around her, things she hadn't noticed because of the spell of Mr. Kirby's words — things like dying sunlight filtering through the trees, the chant of whippoorwills anticipating darkness, dust crowding the shoes of a little girl who somehow felt the world wasn't as black as it had seemed just a little while before.

Mr. Kirby cleared his throat, a little self-consciously. "Well, we better be getting back. Reckon I've bent your ear enough for a while."

"I — I *liked* it," Katty Lou said, hoping the words sounded as sincere as she meant them to. She thought of the question that had been prickling in her mind like a cocklebur for a long time. Perhaps there would never be as good a chance as this. "Mr. Kirby?" she said timidly.

He looked down at her. "Yes, girl?"

"Why did they arrest Homer March?" The minute the question was out she was terrified. If the answer was something awful, she didn't want to know it.

Mr. Kirby was silent for a while, then he said, "He was accused of stealing." Katty Lou held back a gasp of dismay and Mr. Kirby went on. "But that wasn't what he'd done." He draped an arm over a tree branch. "It's quite a story. You see, two or three years ago the Marches sold a man a horse — man from over near Molalla. Fine horse. Cost about two hundred and fifty. Well, in a couple of weeks or so the word got around that the horse had thrown the man. Either that or he fell off. Anyhow, he got mad at the horse and tied it up and whipped it till he drew blood. After that, of course, the horse was scared of him and acted up every time the man came near him. And every time he acted up the man would whip him again.

"Well, when Homer heard about it, he didn't say anything to anybody. Just went to the bank and drew out two hundred and fifty dollars and headed for this man's place. When he found him he flung the money on the ground — all those bills — and said, 'There's your money, mister. I'm taking the horse back. You aren't fit to own a snake, let alone a horse.' Well then, the man — big hulking fellow too — made the mistake of trying to stop him from taking the horse, and Homer, who'd been holding himself in as best he could, just

111

purely blew his top. He beat the living daylights out of the fellow, loaded the horse in the trailer and took off for home.

"He hadn't much more than got there when the law showed up. The man had accused him of stealing the horse. They hauled him off to the sheriff's office. Well, to make a long story short, when the sheriff — he's a horseman himself — heard Homer's side of the story he shook his head and told him to go home and said he wished he had the authority to throw the other man in jail instead."

Katty Lou would have liked to go on thinking about the story, repeating it to herself for a long time, but there was something else she had to ask, something terribly important. She was so eager to ask it that it took almost no time at all to get up the nerve. "Mr. Kirby — couldn't you tell Mrs. Kirby that Homer — well, I mean she doesn't like horses because of her brother and all that, but — but the Marches aren't that way and —"

As her voice trailed off Mr. Kirby shifted his feet uncomfortably. He too seemed to feel the need of getting up his nerve. At last he said, a little desperately, and a little sheepishly, "I tried, girl,

I tried. But — maybe you've noticed — Mrs. Kirby is a pretty strong-minded woman. She's a fine woman, you understand. But — well — we've all got our faults. Mine is liking things to be quiet and peaceful — more than I should, I guess, but that's the way I am. Hers is judging people a little more harshly than maybe they deserve sometimes. But when it comes to trying to change her way of thinking, I —" With his pipe in his hand, he made a helpless sort of gesture. "Well — I guess I'm just getting too old to make the effort. Specially when — part of the time anyway — she may be right and me wrong."

That night Katty Lou lay awake a long time, thinking of all the things Mr. Kirby had told her, but mostly about Homer March and the man who had been cruel to the horse. It was exactly, she decided, what she would have done herself if she had been a man like Homer.

Some time later, as sleep was about to overtake her, she found herself remembering in an idle, sleepy way Mr. Kirby's smoking and the soap. It seemed as if the thought that came then wasn't really hers at all it merely appeared in completed form, like a box of crackers on a grocery shelf.

The thought was this: If the smell of tobacco smoke could be washed off a person with soap, so could the smell of Shetland ponies.

It was the beginning of a struggle with her conscience — a struggle the end of which she knew, in a guilty, spine-tingling way, from the very beginning.

10

IN the deceitful, glorious weeks that followed there was only one dark cloud to mar the sky for Katty Lou. It appeared whenever, without intending to, she found herself thinking of Miss O'Connor. Deceiving and disobeying Mrs. Kirby didn't seem to bother her as much as it should, but when she remembered she was doing the same thing to Miss O'Connor, her conscience came fiendishly to life and tormented her unmercifully. But she couldn't stop doing what she was doing. She was on a toboggan slide of bliss, and there wasn't any way to stop it and get off.

Her decision to take the path of wrongdoing had been made the very night the thought of it came to her, though she kept telling herself that it hadn't, that at the last minute something strong and noble within her would raise a stern, commanding hand and stop her. All the next day, which was Sunday, she told herself the same thing, and even managed to believe it. On Monday morning she was still telling it to herself, though she found she was having trouble meeting Mrs. Kirby's eyes as they ate breakfast. She was telling it up until the very moment Mrs. Kirby said goodbye and started off on her week-day errand of mercy.

Five minutes later Katty Lou, telling herself that nothing was really going to happen, that she was only going through certain motions, like in a pantomime, took down from a nail in the chicken house an old blue denim jacket of Mr. Kirby's and put it on. When she put it back, some of the smell of ponies would stay on it instead of on her. The soap was already taken care of. In the pump house she had found a bar that Mr. Kirby used when he had been tinkering with machinery. She had even tasted it and found it so vile that she almost wished it were necessary for her to wash her mouth with it, as Mr. Kirby had done when he was a boy. That would be a sort of penance for the evil she was about to commit.

Then, moving in a kind of hypnotic state as if

compelled by forces beyond her control, she went through the orchard, across the road and along the creek into the March pasture. She was going to break Tipsy to the halter.

A minute or so later she saw him prancing by his mother's side, full of the clumsy grace and the heartbreaking beauty of young things, and in that instant she forgot — at least for a while — that there were such things in the world as consciences and wrongdoing.

Tipsy snorted at her and sidled off when she came into the pasture. She didn't look like herself in the faded old jacket. It hung to her knees and would have swallowed up her hands if she hadn't rolled the sleeves up. Never having smelled chickens before, he snorted again when he sniffed at it.

As she bent and snapped the lead rope to the halter ring she said soothingly, "You're not going to like this much, but it isn't going to hurt at all — and you've got to learn."

She was right. He didn't like it. As she pulled gently on the rope he looked surprised. Then he jerked his head. When the tension didn't ease he jerked again, harder. Next he tried to run away from whatever it was that held him, and because the rope kept him from running in a straight line, he ran in circles.

Spinning like a top to keep the rope from winding around her as if she were a Maypole, Katty Lou was beginning to be dizzy when Tipsy seemed to realize he wasn't getting anywhere. He stopped abruptly.

Laughing breathlessly and still holding the rope, she went up to him and petted him. After a while he would come along almost willingly, if she didn't lead him too far from Pepper. When she did he would plant all four feet, stiffen his tiny legs and sound his high-pitched, babyish neigh. She would drag him a few feet, surprised each time to feel how strong he was, just to show him he couldn't have his own way. Then she would lead him back to Pepper.

She should have thought about his cries — and Pepper's anxious replies — reaching other ears. She jumped when Homer March's voice spoke quietly behind her. "You're doing a good job there."

She threw him a quick smile and looked away again. She was tense with fear that he might say something about having come to the Kirby house

to look for her. But he didn't. Neither did he say anything about the strange way she was dressed. He merely nodded toward Pepper and said. "Vacation's about over for this gal. She has to work this afternoon. Pony drill." The dismay must have showed in Katty Lou's eyes, because he added quickly, "She'll be back here in the morning."

He walked to Pepper, slapped her affectionately on the neck, and unhooked her chain. Holding onto her halter with one hand, he called offhandedly to Katty Lou. "Come here a second, will you?" She came to his side and suddenly his free arm slid around her, swept her into the air, and she found herself sitting on Pepper's back.

Before she could move or speak he had taken Tipsy's lead rope off, passed it under Pepper's throat and handed the ends to Katty Lou. "There," he said. "She'll handle as well with that as she would with a bridle."

A wild exultation bubbled up inside Katty Lou. She felt bigger than life size. Never in her life had she been mounted on anything but a merry-go-round horse, and seldom that.

Homer stepped back, smiling with satisfaction. "Go on — ride her around a little." He clicked with his tongue, Pepper's ears pricked forward, and all at once, miraculously, Katty Lou was riding.

"Just go around me in a circle," Homer said, his voice giving her confidence. "To go right, lay the left rein against her neck, the opposite to go left. Sit straight and don't lean forward and squeeze with your legs — that's the signal to canter, and you'd better have a saddle when you try that."

Thus began Katty Lou's first riding lesson. Around and around the circle she went, reversing now and then at Homer's direction, stopping and starting. Tipsy trotted along by his mother's flank, making shrill, worried cries. Never before had he seen her make these bewildering movements with a two-legged thing on her back.

It ended at last because Homer beckoned to Katty Lou. She walked Pepper right up to him and said "Ho!" Pepper stopped, patiently waiting for the next thing that might be required of her. That was the strange thing about Homer March. Katty Lou didn't think about it until afterward, but when she did she knew it was so — animals and people alike did what Homer told them to, not because he was Homer but because there seemed never the shadow of a doubt in his mind that what he asked to be done would be done. Because he knew it would be done it *was* done. If he had said, "Katty Lou, get on your pony and jump the Willamette River," she would have jumped it or drowned. Of course she wouldn't have drowned, because Homer never asked the impossible of man, horse or child. He knew what each of them could do, he wanted each to do the best that was in him, but no more. He wanted a good horse to be no better than its rider and a bad horse to be no worse. It went even further than that — as Katty Lou came to know. There weren't any good horses or bad horses, good people or bad ones. There were only people and animals who had been set in wrong ways, or in right ways, by their handling. None of them, given the proper handling, was ever beyond a cure.

Homer was smiling as she rode up and stopped. "Like it?" he asked.

"Oh, yes!" she said, and immediately thought how silly and meaningless the words were. She didn't know that she needn't have answered at all, that the ecstasy shining from her eyes was answer enough.

"Want to help me with something?" he said.

She nodded her reply. "I've got to bring the other ponies up," he went on, "and have them ready for the kids. You can help. Just ride on up to the barn."

"Oh, but I —" She hadn't expected this and she grasped desperately for a reason why she couldn't do it. "There's nobody around to help me," Homer said quickly. "The others had to go to town."

"Oh," she said, not realizing how plainly her relief showed. "I — I'd like to help."

"Good girl!" Homer said. "Let's go."

That was the beginning of the good days. Katty Lou counted as lost every hour she wasn't at the March place and dreaded week ends when she had to stay home all day because Mrs. Kirby was there. She never failed to wash thoroughly and change her clothes after each visit. As often as not she took a complete bath, just to be on the safe side.

For a while she found excuses to go back to the hiding place when Cal and old Evan were around, but gradually her fear of them disappeared. They treated her with casual friendliness, just as if there was nothing wrong with her at all.

She was even able to talk to them a little. But

it was with Homer that the words began to pour from her in ever greater volume, like water through a break in a dike. She talked to him as she had never talked to anyone in her life — even Miss O'Connor. She followed him as he went about his work, asking endless questions, learning more each day about horses and their care and handling. She helped him with every task her strength was equal to — and attempted some it wasn't. She led ponies and horses where he needed them, held them while he saddled or harnessed them. She helped curry them. Because her fingers were quick, she took over almost completely the job of braiding red and white ribbons into the manes of Fandango and Rumba, the matched black Morgans who were used often in parades in nearby towns. She ran a hundred errands a day for Homer and wished there was time to run a hundred more.

11

IT was mid-July and the disobedient life was nearly three weeks along when Katty Lou found Homer in the barn one morning taking the pony carts out. "Hi," he said, with his welcoming smile. "Are you handy with a paintbrush?"

"Sure," Katty Lou said promptly, though she wasn't at all sure. "Are we going to paint the carts?"

"Yep. Got to make 'em shine like a new dime. The big show in Salem's a week from Saturday."

"Oh," she said, a little dismayed. She had heard about the horse show in which the pony drill team would appear, but she thought it was still a long way off. She had had a faint but stubborn hope that some miracle would happen — a miracle that would make it possible for her to go. There wasn't much time now for miracles.

Homer gave her her choice of painting the red

or the white parts, and she chose the red. They lined the carts up in the long passageway in front of the horse stalls and set to work. After a while Katty Lou asked, "Will Tipsy go too?"

"Sure," Homer said. "It's a two-day show, and he can't do without Pepper yet. Not for quite a while."

"What will he do while Pepper's drilling?" she asked anxiously, fearing that Tipsy might be left alone and unhappy in a stall.

"Oh, he'll go right along," Homer said. "Matter of fact, he'll be the hit of the show."

"Won't he get in the way when they do the figure-eights and things?" Her concern was not that the drill might be spoiled but that Tipsy might be hurt.

"Here's how it'll work," Homer said. With his finger he drew a large oval in the dust on the barn floor. "That's the ring where we perform. Here at the side is where we come in when we get the signal. All right — Pepper's the lead horse, so she'll be out first, and right beside her will be Tipsy, with one of the kids leading him. They start off to the right and circle clear around the ring before they line up here in the center for the drill. Whoever's leading Tipsy will take him over to the side here where he'll be out of the way. Then at the wind-up he'll go out with her."

Katty Lou was silent for a while, her eyes dreamy and a little wistful as she pictured Tipsy in the show ring, cheered by thousands of people. She was so deep in the dream that Homer's voice startled her. "Katty Lou —" The seriousness in his voice made her uneasy and she looked at him sharply. His eyes were on his work and his paint-brush swished steadily over the gleaming white cart shaft. "I haven't ever said anything about this. Had no cause to. But now I have. It's just that — well, I've put two and two together and I know why you never come here on week ends and why you always scat out about twelve-thirty —"

Katty Lou had stopped painting, her face hot as fire, and she didn't dare look at him.

"I only mention it," he hurried on, "so you'll know why I don't just waltz across the road and say, 'Mrs. Kirby, I sure would like to take Katty Lou to the Salem show.' But I know that wouldn't do because she would know you've been coming here. That's right, isn't it?"

She could only nod miserably and he went on.

"Isn't there something we could do? Just say I'm taking all the kids in the neighborhood — something like that?"

Katty Lou shook her head quickly and said in a small voice, "I — I'd be afraid to. It might spoil everything."

He sighed. "Well, all right. But don't give up. Maybe I'll think of something yet." He didn't sound very confident.

There were two more practice sessions before the day of the show. As always, when the first of the young drivers arrived, Katty Lou disappeared. She was simply not able to face them. When they were actually out in the ring drilling, though, she slipped from the hiding place into the barn to comfort Tipsy, who was shut up in a box stall during Pepper's absence. He needed a lot of comforting because he didn't like being away from his mother one bit, and he said so, shrilly and repeatedly.

The last practice was on Friday, the day before the show opened — the day the miracle happened. It was a miracle with a slow fuse that sputtered for a long time.

Homer rushed the boys and girls through the drill that afternoon and dismissed them early. Then he began loading the carts into the big truck along with all the harnesses, oats, bales of hay and other things that would be needed. He was to take the load to the state fairgrounds in Salem that afternoon, then make another trip in the evening for the ponies. Katty Lou helped with the harnesses and whatever else she could carry, but her usual eagerness was lacking and she was even a tiny bit resentful that Homer went at his work so lightheartedly. She told herself she was being silly, that there was no reason why he shouldn't be gay. He enjoyed the show as much as any of the children.

When twelve-thirty came she gave Tipsy a last, lingering hug and told him to be a good pony and not cause trouble. To Homer she said, "Well — I've got to go. I hope — I hope everything goes fine."

That was the moment the fuse began to splutter.

Homer looked at her with a mischievous light in his eyes. "So long, nymph," he said cheerfully. "See you at the ringside."

She stared at him uncomprehendingly. "What — what did you say?"

He rubbed a finger along the side of his nose and winked. "Didn't say a word," he said. "Not a word." Off he went, whistling gaily, with an armload of horse blankets. There was nothing she could do about it because she had to hurry home and wash away the telltale smell of horse.

The fuse smoldered on until it burned to the powder keg at supper that night. Mrs. Kirby had been chattering happily, telling about her patient, Mrs. Armishaw. Mrs. Armishaw had taken a turn for the better and soon, perhaps, wouldn't require so much care. Mrs. Kirby could then give more attention to Katty Lou, whom she felt she had been neglecting.

Ordinarily this news would have made Katty Lou distinctly uncomfortable, knowing that soon her precious hours of freedom might end, but tonight she was hardly aware of what was being said. She could think only that the pony show was about to happen and that she would have no part in it, she who had done so much toward getting ready for it.

She was even feeling a little sorry for herself —

something she almost never did — when the powder keg exploded.

She was aware suddenly that Mrs. Kirby had broken off her account of the ills of Mrs. Armishaw and was looking directly at Katty Lou with a smile. She was saying, "I almost forgot, dear. Mr. Kirby has a kind of surprise for you. Arthur — you tell her."

"Well," Mr. Kirby said, wiping his mouth with what seemed unnecessary thoroughness, "I've got a little business to tend to down at Salem in the morning. I thought you might like to go along." He paused, and Katty Lou, who was watching every movement of his face, saw a twinkle appear in his pale blue eyes. "And then," he went on, "I thought we might take in the big horse show at the fairgrounds. Think you'd like that?"

Katty Lou didn't know that her eyes were as big as silver dollars nor that her lips had parted suddenly to take in a rush of breath. She knew only that at any moment she might explode like a stick of dynamite and disappear, leaving nothing but a little purple cloud. She didn't know how long it was before she remembered she was expected to say something. After that it seemed forever before she could manage to say, in a voice so faint she could scarcely hear it herself, "Yes — oh yes — I would!"

She went through the motions of listening — though she didn't actually hear a bit of it — to Mrs. Kirby's explanation of how she hadn't even considered letting Katty Lou go to the horse show until she learned that Mr. and Mrs. Bayliss were going, and you could be sure that anything Sam and Laura Bayliss went to was perfectly all right because Sam was a fine man, and Laura . . .

12

THEY started off in the old Chevrolet right after breakfast.

Mr. Kirby was dressed in what he called his "good" suit, though it was the only suit he owned. Katty Lou was wearing her blue quilted skirt and yellow blouse. Because she had worn nothing but jeans for so long the skirt felt strange but rather gay, as if she were dressed up for a party. Mr. Kirby seemed to feel gay too. He turned from the driveway into the road and began to accelerate. "We're off!" he said exultantly, and looked sideways at Katty Lou with a twinkle in his eyes.

Katty Lou felt like echoing, "We're off!" but didn't quite have the nerve. Then it occurred to her that she wouldn't have hesitated if Mr. Kirby was Homer March. Thinking of Homer made her wonder again, as she had been doing ever since the evening before, just what he had done to bring about the miracle of Mr. Kirby's invitation. That Homer was behind it somehow there could be no doubt, because it was obvious now that he had known Mr. Kirby was going to take her to the show.

A moment later it seemed as though she must have been doing her thinking out loud. Suddenly Mr. Kirby said, "Y'know, I wouldn't even have thought of going to this horse show if it hadn't been for young March."

"Oh?" said Katty Lou, trying to sound surprised.

"Ran into him at the feed store," Mr. Kirby went on. "Matter of fact" — here he took one hand off the wheel and scratched his head reflectively — "I sort of got the idea he followed me down there — but of course that's a silly notion. Anyhow, we got to talking and he told me he was going to show some horses and ponies and one thing or another, and that it was a real first-class show and I ought to come along and bring the family. Well, I was saying I didn't see how I could manage it when he hauled out some white ribbons that say 'Exhibitor' on them and said, 'These'll get you in free and they don't cost me a cent.' " Mr. Kirby chuckled. "I'm a sucker for anything that's free, but I was still doubtful about driving forty miles and back just to see a show. That young March, though — he could talk a policeman out of his brass buttons if he put his mind to it, and he kept at it."

Katty Lou smiled, picturing a policeman handing his buttons to Homer March.

"Just then," Mr. Kirby went on, "I remembered this business I've got to take care of at the state agriculture office, and that made up my mind." He chuckled again. "Of course, the business could've waited a month or so — but I always say, never put off till tomorrow what you'd rather do today."

Because of his high spirits Mr. Kirby talked on and on. Something was always reminding him of another subject. A horse in a field made him think of the days when he was "a young sprout" and drove a team hauling cordwood. A passing logging truck reminded him of his years as a logger, after the first World War. Katty Lou was content to let him do the talking. She couldn't have talked about anything but the horse show, which wouldn't have been very satisfactory because she had never seen one and had no idea of what, aside from the pony drill, would be going on.

In an hour they were driving into Salem and soon Katty Lou caught a glimpse of the great round cupola of the state capitol, blindingly white in the sunlight and topped by the golden statue of the Pioneer. She knew what it was from the many pictures she had seen. A few minutes later she was walking beside Mr. Kirby up the steps of one of the big state office buildings, all built of the same white marble as the capitol itself.

They found the office Mr. Kirby was looking for and Katty Lou sat on a bench while he talked to a man at a long counter. He talked to the man a long time and then began filling out forms the man gave him. There was nothing for Katty Lou to do but stare at a huge map of Oregon on the wall opposite her. Red, yellow and white pins were stuck into the map, singly and in clusters. She wondered what the pins were for, but didn't really care.

It was a long wait, but she didn't mind. She was too busy thinking about the horse show, and pictures of it — as she imagined it — chased in and out of her mind.

At last Mr. Kirby finished his business and they went to a drive-in for lunch. The restaurant was near the fairgrounds, Mr. Kirby said. The first thing Katty Lou saw when they sat down at the counter was a booth full of young girls. One of them couldn't have been much older than Katty Lou. All of them were dressed in beautifully tailored riding habits with the round derby hats that she had seen before only in books.

"Contestants in the show, sure enough," said Mr. Kirby. "And look over there — cowboys!" He pointed to another booth in which four young men were eating enthusiastically. Burned by the sun and wind, their faces were a deep mahogany. They all wore faded jeans, bright-colored shirts and high-heeled boots, and around each muscular neck was a gay wisp of neckerchief, knotted at the side. Mr. Kirby said, "Bet they're out for calf-roping money."

The excitement that had been merely simmering inside Katty Lou now began to boil. She could eat only half of the hamburger and part of the strawberry milkshake Mr. Kirby had bought her. The excitement was nearly unbearable when they reached the fairgrounds and drove into the parking area near the huge white building that housed the show ring on one side and on the other the stalls for hundreds of animals. The parking area was crowded with colorful horse trailers, some hitched to trucks in matching colors. And everywhere were horses. Katty Lou had never dreamed there could be so many — or so many riders in handsome costumes — or so many saddles and bridles gleaming with inlaid silver. Many of the riders were in the exercise ring at the side of the arena, warming up their horses for the show.

As they started toward the main entrance, Mr. Kirby produced the two white ribbons with gold letters that spelled Exhibitor. "Here," he said, "you pin 'em onto us. I'm not much of a hand at pinning."

Ordinarily deft with her hands, Katty Lou fumbled awkwardly as she pinned one ribbon to his lapel with trembling fingers and the other to her blouse. Inside the arena they found most of the seats already occupied and she felt a touch of panic, fearing there might be none left for them. But she should have counted on Homer. "Come on," Mr. Kirby said, taking her hand, "he told me just where to sit — over there by the entrance where the performers come in."

He led Katty Lou to the side of the arena and seated her in the front row, just above the big gates which would be swung open to admit the first riders into the ring. The air was electric with the deep-throated hum of hundreds of voices in the grandstand and the neighing of excited horses from the stable area below and to the rear of where they were sitting. Now and then came the shouted "Hah!" of a man reprimanding an unruly horse. Once Katty Lou even thought she heard Tipsy's high-pitched call, but she couldn't be sure.

By looking down and to the side she could see along the passageway through which the performers would come and into a part of the stable area where people and horses were milling about in an almost tangible aura of mounting excitement. Her own excitement was at such a pitch that she didn't realize for a moment that Mr. Kirby was speaking to her. He had bought a program and was holding it open in front of her and saying, "See — right here — Number seven." She looked, and there after the big numeral 7 was the heading THE MARCH KIDS PONY DRILL. Sight of the printed words somehow added to her excitement. She felt

139

as if she couldn't possibly wait for the moment when Tipsy would trot out at the head of the little cavalcade.

Fortunately something happened the very next instant to divert her. The plop of many hoofs on the hard-packed sawdust of the passageway beside her sounded suddenly loud and close. With it was the creak of saddles and the subdued voices of men. She whirled and there, just on a level with her eyes, was an American flag held in a stirrup holster by a man on a black horse. He wore gray-blue trousers and a shirt decorated with bright red and yellow piping and a broad-brimmed yellow Stetson. Behind him was another man dressed the same way, also on a black horse and also holding a flag in his left hand. Behind him were another and another as far back as she could see.

Suddenly, from hidden amplifiers, a fanfare of trumpets burst forth — ta-ta-ta-*ta* ta-*ta!* — and then a man's voice — "Ladies and gentlemen — our national anthem!" An instant later the big gates at Katty Lou's right were jerked open by two big boys. An unseen band swung into the first notes of the anthem. As though launched by a catapult the first black horse in the line burst into the arena and swung sharply to the left, the bright flag rippling with the speed of his going. A second later the next horse and rider leaped out, swinging to the right. The third followed the first, the fourth followed the second. In no time at all two swift-moving lines of flag-bearing horsemen were circling the arena in opposite directions at a swift canter, the drumming of their hoofs muted only a little by the music. The audience, as though jerked by strings in an unseen hand, was on its feet cheering wildly. Katty Lou wasn't cheering. She was on her feet, but in the first moment all breath had left her and she couldn't have made a sound to save her life.

Then, almost before she could believe it was happening, the two lines of riders had whirled, forming up abreast on either side of the ring. They dashed forward, passing through each other's ranks in the center of the ring, and stopped, a line facing each side of the grandstand. There they stood, as still as equestrian statues, until the anthem was over. They remained standing while the announcer's voice came over the amplifier. "Ladies and gentlemen, please be seated. Welcome to the eleventh annual Salem horse show — and may I

141

remind you there will be another performance tonight at eight and another tomorrow afternoon at this time. And now — on with the show!"

After that, things happened so fast that later, when Katty Lou tried to recreate in her mind every cherished detail, she found that much of it had become a confused blur of sights, sounds, colors and impressions. There were the judging

events, which were particularly hard to keep straight in her mind. There were so many of them, and so many men, women and children competing in them. Their names were strange to her too — Equitation, English pleasure horses, Western pleasure horse, Driving horses (formal), Roadster to bike, Three-gaited class, Trail horses, and many others.

Then there were the exhibition events, which were easier to remember because they were more exciting. The calf roping was one, though she couldn't help feeling sorry for the calves as the whistling ropes flipped them over on their sides before they could run even half the arena's length. While the canny cow pony kept the rope taut, each

rider flung himself from the saddle and seemed almost to slide down the rope to the helpless calf. Frantically he threw a hitch of rope around three of the calf's feet and then sprang back, throwing his arms into the air as a signal to the timer that he was finished.

Another was an exhibition of "dressage" by a man riding the most beautiful palomino Katty Lou had ever seen. By the hush that fell over the audience while the man and horse performed, and by the thunderous applause at the end, she knew she was seeing something rare and wonderful. The man, in his black formal habit with the snowy white stock at his neck and the derby hat, sat the horse like a waxen image. For all anyone could see, he never moved a muscle or uttered a sound, and yet the beautiful golden stallion went through a more complex set of movements, steps and maneuvers than many an accomplished human dancer could have done. At times he seemed to skip like a happy child, at others he moved with a stately grace like a grand duke leading a quadrille. He went through the steps of the walk, trot and canter without ever leaving the spot he was in, and then he was moving not forward or sideways but both at the same time, the left hind foot stepping unerringly each time on the spot just vacated by the right forefoot. It was magic, poetry, dancing and horsemanship all offered up in one breath-taking, beautiful package. In a way, Katty Lou thought, it was a horse being more than a horse, and a man being more than a man. Neither the man nor the horse by himself could even have begun to achieve anything so lovely, yet the horse and the man together seemed to create something that was more than the sum of the two of them. Often in lonely hours later she tried to think back and to put her finger on just what sort of magic they made, but always the thing eluded her, leaving her with only the certainty that what she had seen that day was something seldom seen in an imperfect world — perfection.

Even that event, much as she loved to think back on it later, became a humdrum affair in comparison with the amazing, unbelievable, terrifying, glorious thing that happened just as the sixth event was ending and Number 7 about to begin.

In her absorption with what went on in the ring, she lost track of the events by their numbers. She was watching as the winners of the three-gaited class rode forward in turn to receive their ribbons from the judges, when all at once a familiar voice sounded in her right ear. "Hi, nymph. How do you like the show?" Her head jerked around, and there, not two feet away, was the smiling face of Homer March.

Startled, she gave a little gasp. Only his head and shoulders showed above the railing between her and the passageway. He was standing on a ladder fastened to the grandstand wall just beside the gate. The ladder, like the one on the opposite side of the passageway, was for exhibitors and performers who wanted to join their friends in the grandstand when they weren't needed behind the scenes. "Got a friend of yours here," Homer went on, nodding toward the ground below him. Katty Lou leaned over the railing, looked down and gasped again. There was Tipsy wearing a red and white ribbon around his neck, tied in a bowknot just behind his ears. He was crowding close to Pepper's flank as she stood between the shafts of her cart, the other carts lined up behind her.

Tipsy's topknot fairly bristled with worry and he kept nosing against Pepper's side, only to be balked each time by the unfriendly hardness of the shaft. He couldn't understand what this strange thing was that stood between him and the warmth and softness of his mother. Pepper too was worried. She kept trying to turn and look at him, but each time her young driver twitched the opposite rein, as was proper, and brought her head forward again. She had work to do, as Katty Lou knew quite well, and shouldn't be allowed to think of other things. Yet when it came to Tipsy, Katty Lou simply couldn't be as stern as Homer always said you had to be if you were to make a good horse out of a smart horse. She could even remember his words: "More horses have been ruined by too much kindness than have been ruined by the lack of it. You don't ever do an animal a favor by spoiling it. You ask a horse to work hard, you ask him to work intelligently, and if he doesn't want to do it — which he probably won't — you *make* him do it. He'll either fight you or he'll try to outsmart you — if he doesn't he's no good — but if you're the right kind of rider for him, and that means only one kind of rider — the one who's boss — you'll find yourself with a horse that will do just

what you want it to, and at the *time* you want it
to, not five minutes later. Not when it gets good
and ready to."

Katty Lou had heard him speak of these things
so many times that the words and phrases went
around in her mind as if they were on a phono-
graph record: "You'll be told, and you'll hear, and
you'll see, a lot of things about horses that are just
plain lies. They're lies made up by people who've
never been any closer to a horse than I've been to
the Queen of England. They'll tell you that a horse
who's running free will come when his master
whistles. That's a lie. Some horses will come to a
whistle, but they're trick horses, not working
horses. A working horse will come to a whistle
only if he's got good reason to believe the whistle
has some oats connected with it. They'll tell you
a horse will face a mortal danger to save its master. That's another lie — one of the worst of the
lies. A horse is like every other living thing. It's
first job — its *duty*, you might say — is to stay alive,
and it's going to stay alive no matter how many
men in fancy pants are whistling at it to come and
kill a snake, or trample a bad man. A horse doesn't
know a good man from a bad one. How could he?

He only knows that one man feeds him and another doesn't. One man's kind to him and another isn't. And he gets a little leery of the lot of them. I've never mistreated a horse in my life, but I've yet to see one that'll come of its own free will and sit in my lap because of the kindness of my heart. They want as little to do with me as possible, because I'm the guy who makes them do what it's not their nature to do. They won't thank me for it, they won't love me for it, and they won't come and save my life because of it. It's up to me to save my own life, and it's up to them to save theirs. Sometimes I can help them, but only because I'm a little smarter than they are, and because I know better than they do what's good for them. Don't ever believe a word of this rot you'll hear about a horse being grateful for what's done for him. He's not. There's no such thing as gratitude in a horse. He's only an animal, an intelligent animal — and he's probably the most beautiful one on earth — but he's not your mother or your father or your sister Sue. He'll serve you because he has to — if he's been properly trained — but he'll never love you and he'll never save your life except accidentally, in the saving of his own. Don't count on

149

the horse to love *you*, kids. Just *you* love *him*, and the rest will take care of itself."

No, it was wrong for Pepper to look around while she was in harness, and Katty Lou knew it. All the same she couldn't help feeling sorry for the mare, and for Tipsy too. She longed to go down and comfort him, tell him that nothing was going to hurt him.

Homer might almost have been reading her mind, for he said, "We've got a minute yet. Come on down and pet the little fella. He's used to you and it might calm him down."

The eagerness that surged up in her died quickly as she glanced at Pepper's driver and the driver behind him. She couldn't possibly go down there in front of the eyes of all those children. "No," she said, "I — I couldn't —"

Homer paid no attention. "Oh come on," he said. "It'll be all right." Before she knew what was happening, his big arm had reached out, scooped her up and was lifting her over the railing. In a moment she was on the ground beside Tipsy and there was nothing to do but put her arms around him, hug him tight and frantically pretend no one was looking at her. She even closed her eyes as she hugged him, so she didn't see when Homer snapped Tipsy's lead rope to his halter.

She did look up in sudden fright as the gates creaked open and the winners of the last event came riding through. Even that, though, was nothing to what she felt when the announcer's voice boomed out — "And now, ladies and gentlemen, a very *special* event — The March Kids Pony Drill!"

Then it happened. Katty Lou found herself standing bolt upright, rigid as iron, with Homer kneeling by her side, hugging her as tight as she had been hugging Tipsy. His other hand was closing hers over the end of Tipsy's rope. His lips were close to her ear but his voice seemed to come from far away. "He's yours, Katty Lou. You saw him first. You get to show him first. Once around the ring, like I said, and then lead him straight to me. That's all there is to it."

Words seemed to tear themselves loose from a throat that didn't want to let them out. "No — no — no I *can't*." She tried to let go of the rope but his big hand closed over hers and held it tight.

"You *can*, Katty Lou, you *can*." His voice was steady, calm, and firm. "Listen to me, Katty Lou.

You've got nothing in the world to be afraid of — nothing to be ashamed of — not one thing. You're the prettiest girl in the place, and I wish you belonged to me. Now — you're going out there and do this — for me — and I'm going to be proud of you."

He was standing now. His hand, in the middle of her back, was pushing her gently, relentlessly forward, and somehow her feet were moving, though there was no sensation in them. The arena loomed before her like a vast and frightening desert. One last time she heard his voice — urgent, commanding. "Go now — to the right — and walk fast!"

How she did it she would never know, because of course it was utterly impossible for her to step out in full view of those hundreds of watching eyes. She had no doubt of what would happen. She would die.

Perhaps it was because Tipsy suddenly pulled back on his rope. Automatically, without thinking, because she had done it so many times before, she stepped forward, pulling him along. After that it was like a strange dream — the kind of dream she had often had, in which she knew she was dreaming and seemed to stand aside and watch herself doing it, as though she was not really herself at all.

At first she wondered about the strange roaring in her ears. Maybe it was the way you felt when you began to die. After what seemed a very long time she realized the roaring didn't come from inside her head but from the people in the grandstand. They were cheering and clapping, and she was already rounding the curve at the end of the oval ring.

Suddenly a little child's voice — high and piercing — separated itself from the general uproar. "Oh — Mommie! He's *darling!*"

The child was talking about Tipsy, of course, and Katty Lou wondered in a curiously detached way why she hadn't thought of it before. That was what the cheering was about — and all those eyes weren't watching *her,* they were watching him. And they were loving him, just as she had done from the moment she first set eyes on him. Suddenly she felt a kind of pity for all those people in the grandstand because *they* hadn't been there in the dew-damp grass the morning he was born. *They* hadn't seen him struggle to his feet and take

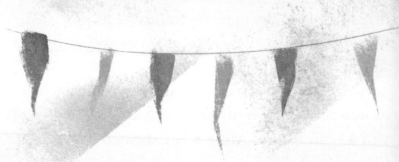

the first step of his life. They hadn't taught him to come along when his rope was pulled, nor scratched his hard little head, nor held his soft neck in their arms, and they never would. They were privileged to watch him only for a few short minutes, while *she* would be with him again

and again — watching him grow, watching him learn. . . .

For the first time she turned her head, quite unself-consciously, and looked at him. His head was up, his tiny ears were pricked forward and his feet in their little stockings danced along as confidently

as if he were a gray old veteran of many shows. Katty Lou knew, of course, that he wouldn't have been that way if his mother weren't a step or two behind him, but she wasn't thinking of that. She was thinking only that he was fine and brave and beautiful, even if he wasn't any bigger than a fair-sized dog. She was proud of him, so proud that the pride came up in her throat and squeezed it.

All unbidden, then, came some of the last words she had heard. "You're going to go out there and do this — for me — and I'm going to be proud of you." Homer! Homer — without whom she would never have known Tipsy as she did, without whom there would have been nothing for her but another day — and another and another, each one just like the last. He was going to be proud of her, just as she was proud of Tipsy. Unconsciously her chin came up an inch or two, her back straightened and she looked across the ring toward the gates where she had left him — she was directly opposite them now. But he wasn't by the gates. He was standing in the middle of the ring, straighter and taller than ever in his white Western outfit with its red piping and embroidery and his huge white hat.

Katty Lou smiled at him — a shy flicker of a smile — and she walked a little faster, holding Tipsy's rope with a firm and confident hand.

She didn't know of course that all this time Homer March had never taken his eyes from her and that when she smiled he took a slow and mighty breath. For the first time, one by one, his muscles softened, easing gradually the steel-hard tension that had gripped them from the moment he pushed her out into the ring.

It seemed no time at all — as a matter of fact, astoundingly, it was over all too soon — before she had made the complete circle and was heading toward Homer in the center of the ring. He put his whistle to his mouth, blew a short, sharp blast, and Katty Lou didn't need to turn her head to know what was going on behind her. The drivers drew their ponies up, all abreast in a single line, and faced him. The applause grew deafening and Homer swept the broad hat from his head and bowed, first in one direction, then in another. Standing before him as he bowed, Katty Lou — and no one else — heard him say, "Good girl! I told you I'd be proud of you." She thought she might burst from the pressures inside her, or maybe leave the ground and float into the air to bob against the ceiling like a gas-filled balloon.

When the hat was back on his head he nodded toward the far side of the ring and said in a low voice, "Take him over there against the wall and just stand until the drill's over. Then you lead the way out." He raised his whistle and sent the drill team into the first of its maneuvers.

From then on Katty Lou had her hands too full with Tipsy to think of anything else. He allowed himself to be led to the wall easily enough, but once there and turned around he realized for the first time that Pepper was no longer with him. Instead, she was trotting off in the opposite direction at the head of a column of twinkling-wheeled carts, and he didn't like it a bit. He cried, he bounced, he cavorted, and he cried some more, but the hand that held him never gave way. At last he merely stood by Katty Lou's side, watching the big ponies go by and nickering plaintively. Rubbing his topknot, Katty Lou spoke soft, reassuring words. When the drill was finished at last, the carts were formed up in a line again, and Homer had taken his bow, she started forward with Tipsy in response to Homer's beckoning.

At sight of Tipsy the applause, which had begun to die down, welled up again until it seemed to shake the rafters high above. Katty Lou was smiling up at Homer with a happiness so all-embracing that she didn't even notice the man who ran up from somewhere, pointed his camera and flashed his bulb. He even did it a second time, but all she was aware of was Homer's voice: "Didn't I tell you? He was the hit of the show! Go on, now — lead 'em out."

Proudly she led Tipsy out, feeling as though she weighed an ounce or two less than nothing at all. Passing through the gate, she glanced up, and there was Mr. Kirby, his hat pushed back on his head, hair stringing out from under it. He was wearing a grin too big for his face and he was clapping like a man gone mad.

13

SUNDAY was a difficult day to get through. In a way it made things easier for Katty Lou to know that Homer and the ponies were still in Salem instead of across the road where she couldn't have gone to see them anyway. All she could think of was the show. She followed Mr. Kirby around as he went about his chores just so she could talk about it. There seemed no limit to the number of times she could talk about the same things without getting tired of them.

She went to bed before it was really dark, just to get through with today and bring tomorrow faster. If she had known what tomorrow would bring she would have wished for today to go on forever.

The storm broke at the breakfast table.

Mr. Kirby had finished and left for work. Katty Lou also had finished and was starting to wash the dishes while Mrs. Kirby lingered over her coffee, leafing through the pages of the morning paper. Katty Lou was on pins and needles, scarcely able to contain herself until Mrs. Kirby would be gone and she could hurry to the March place to hear how Tipsy had behaved in the other two shows. Because she was running water into the sink, she didn't hear Mrs. Kirby call her name the first time. She heard the second time, though. Mrs. Kirby's voice was raised slightly, and in some way impossible to explain it sent a chill of fear up Katty Lou's back. She turned off the faucet and stood waiting, looking at nothing, feeling the chill creep over her.

"Katty Lou, will you look at this, please?"

She turned reluctantly and moved on weighted feet toward the kitchen table. Something was wrong. She didn't know what it was, but trouble — bad trouble — seemed to be hovering in the air around her.

Mrs. Kirby didn't look up from the newspaper which lay spread out on the table in front of her but she turned it slowly around so that it was right side up for Katty Lou. Her finger pointed to the middle of the page and she said in a flat tone that could have meant anything, "This. Look at this." It was all the more ominous because Mrs. Kirby was so quiet, because she didn't burst into her usual flood of speech.

With unwilling, frightened eyes Katty Lou looked, and at once the awful truth confronted her. There, in damning black and white, was a photograph of herself and Tipsy and Homer March, with the lineup of ponies behind them. Her face was tilted up toward Homer, who was smiling down at her, and by some improbable sorcery the photographer had captured all the joy, the gratitude and the love that had shone from her eyes in that moment.

Unable to speak, she stared at the photograph until she could no longer see it, and when Mrs. Kirby spoke at last the words seemed to come from far away. "It looks as if you and he are very good friends indeed."

Katty Lou could only go on staring at the printed page on which the words shifted and swam together in meaningless blurs. There was nothing — not a thing in the world — to say. Then came the question she knew would come sooner or later.

"Have you been over there every day while I've been gone?"

Of their own accord Katty Lou's fingers twisted together in front of her. Mutely, miserably, she nodded. Without looking at her, Katty Lou could tell that Mrs. Kirby's eyes were boring into her. Then she said in the sharpest tone Katty Lou had ever heard her use, "I don't see *how* you could do it!"

Words and phrases jostled their way through Katty Lou's mind — that she knew she had done wrong, that she was sorry, dreadfully sorry, that it had all begun because of Tipsy, that she couldn't help herself — but she knew she couldn't say them. No words could hide the fact that she had committed a wickedness and she had been found out.

Soft rustling noises came from Mrs. Kirby as she turned. Then she said, "I haven't time now to decide what to do about this. I have to get over to Mrs. Armishaw's. But one thing will have to be done — I'll have to let Miss O'Connor know about it."

Katty Lou's head had been sinking farther all the time and now her chin touched a button on her skirt. Still the thoughts were racing through her mind and still she could not voice a single one. She heard Mrs. Kirby's step as she moved to the back door where she paused and said tartly, "I suppose I may as well give you permission to go this morning, because you will anyway."

The screen door closed behind her and the dam broke inside Katty Lou. With eyes blinded by sudden tears she stared unseeing toward the door and called out wildly, "No! — Mrs. Kirby! — I won't! — I *won't!*" But there was no reply. Only the sound of footsteps going down the drive.

The day was the longest of Katty Lou's life. All morning she plodded through a list of self-imposed chores, doing her best not to think of anything but what her hands were doing. She gave the kitchen a thorough cleaning, taking all the time she could about it. She even swept and mopped the floor, though it didn't particularly need it. Anything to keep busy, to get through this day somehow. And tomorrow? Tomorrow was a blank, an emptiness, a darkness.

Later, kneeling in the garden, pulling weeds from under the tomato vines, she found herself listening in a strange impersonal way to the sound of a voice. The voice was her own. She was talking softly to Marie Madeleine DuBois, and with a queer kind of feeling she couldn't have explained she realized that she hadn't said a word to Marie Madeleine in a very long time.

In the afternoon Mrs. Kirby mentioned only once the thing that was on both their minds. "I called Miss O'Connor's office," she said, "but she was out of town and won't be there until tomorrow morning." She was careful not to look at Katty Lou when she added, "I've decided to leave it all to her. If she decides you might be better off in another home, then that's the way it will be." Once more, her very quietness was worse than a thousand words.

At supper Mr. Kirby, who didn't know yet that he was sitting at table with a convicted criminal, talked with unusual gaiety. He told a story or two and the others did their best to seem amused. Worst of all, he kept bringing up events at the horse show which had impressed him particularly. Each time Katty Lou writhed inwardly and avoided Mrs. Kirby's eyes. She responded as best she could, in painful monosyllables, and went through the motions of eating, swallowing each bite with enormous effort. The moment the last dish was dried and put away she fled to her room while Mr. Kirby, still in his ignorance, went out to milk Betsy and attend to his other chores. When he came in, she knew he would be informed of her sins.

For a long time it was quiet in the house except for the summer-evening sounds that came in through Katty Lou's open window — the contented murmuring of the chickens, the sad, distant lowing of cattle, the robins' vesper song. Sitting on the edge of her bed, hands folded neatly in her lap, doing nothing, she heard each sound with a strange clarity, as though it had for her some meaning it didn't have for others who might hear. The sounds meant not just the ending of another day but the ending of good things for always and in all places. Then came the high, imperious neigh of a horse, beginning with a scream and ending in a bubbling rumble. Without a doubt it was Gunsmoke, and in her mind Katty Lou could see him fling his proud head high, whirl and run, his black mane billowing like a flag, as far as the stout bars of his corral would let him. The real sound and the imagined sight set off in her mind without warning, like a string of firecrackers, a whole series of other sights, other sounds. They had to do with Gunsmoke and all the other horses and ponies, with old Evan and Cal and Shadow, with pony-cart wheels glinting in the sun. Most of all they had to do with a tiny Shetland colt and a big young man with something more than kindness in his eyes.

The bed creaked gently, twice, as her small body twisted convulsively around and her face and outstretched arms came down against the quilt. Now there was a new sound in the room to signify that more than just another day was ending.

14

LONG after Katty Lou had worn herself out with sobbing and the tears had dried, she lay in a kind of paralysis of misery, wondering dully what would become of her but not really caring. How anything could matter now was beyond her understanding.

What roused her was the sudden flapping of the old window shade and then a puff of chill, moist air where a moment before everything had been still. In a moment there was another puff, blowing cold on her cheeks. Rain was coming. She lay for a while, not caring about that either. Good weather — bad weather. They were the same to her. Then came the sound of Mr. Kirby's feet on the back steps, the slamming of the door as the wind blew it shut behind him. After that the voices began, as she had known they would. She got up stiffly and closed the window.

For a while none of the words reached her. Mr. Kirby's voice was low as always, and Mrs. Kirby was speaking softly too. Besides, the wind was beginning to sigh through the cherry tree outside Katty Lou's window and to murmur along the eaves. She hoped it would blow harder, so that she could hear nothing.

But Mrs. Kirby's voice rose higher, and now and then a word or two reached Katty Lou in spite of everything. Twice she heard the name of Miss O'Connor and each time it made her wince. Then Mrs. Kirby's voice was audible for a moment, but a sudden gust drowned out the words, and Katty Lou sat huddled on the bed wishing she were a thousand miles away — or deaf — or dead.

At last came the sound of the Kirbys' footsteps as they went to their bedroom. The murmur of their voices went on for a while, and then there was silence, except for the swish of the wind and a dull pounding that had started up inside Katty Lou's head. Soon the first raindrops came pelting at her window. Darkness had come.

There was no way of knowing how long she sat there, her body numb, her thoughts racing, turning, getting nowhere, like a mouse in a maze. Time had lost its meaning. She didn't know when the idea came — the idea that told her what she had to do. She didn't stop to think that it wasn't a very good idea. She was beyond thinking clearly anyway. She could think only that it was a way out.

She got off the bed and, groping in the darkness because she was afraid to turn on her light, she began to take her clothes from the closet and dresser and lay them on the bed.

When they were all collected she made a bundle of them, using her old cloth coat to wrap them in. Then she put on her raincoat, which came to just above her knees now, tied a scarf around her head, and was ready to go.

Because the door to the little hall squeaked, she opened it cautiously, an inch at a time. Probably it couldn't have been heard anyway because the rain was drumming steadily on the roof. All the same Katty Lou was careful going down the stairs, staying close to the wall where the boards weren't so likely to squeak. The stairway was as dark as a tomb and she gripped the handrail hard, holding her bundle with the other hand.

At the bottom of the stairs she saw with relief

that no lights were on. Groping her way through the dining room to the kitchen, she felt along the wall at the side of the stove until her hand closed over the flashlight that always hung there. Taking it down, she had a momentary qualm. Was she adding stealing to the list of her crimes? She told herself she would find some way to send it back. Right now she simply couldn't do without it. Switching it on, she held her hand cupped over the light so that only a little showed, and tiptoed back through the dining room and into the living room.

At the front door she stopped, set her bundle down, opened the door, picked up her bundle and slipped through, closing the door behind her with infinite care.

The night was dark. At first Katty Lou could see nothing but the faint gleam of rain on the leaves of the laurel hedge near the road. The wind had eased and the rain was coming down steadily but not hard. Katty Lou didn't mind the rain. It would make things easier — the first thing anyway — the thing she had known from the beginning she would have to do before she went away.

She had to see Tipsy just once more, to say

goodbye. The rain meant that Homer would have put him in the barn — along with Pepper of course — rather than leave him out with the big ponies where he might catch cold. The big ponies would stand and let the rain run off their hairy coats, but Tipsy would get tired and lie down on the wet ground, which would be dangerous at his age.

She let herself out the gate and crossed the road — flashing the light just often enough to make sure she didn't step into the ditch — and started up the March lane. The house was dark and silent,

but all the same she walked at the side of the lane, where there was grass, to avoid the crunching of gravel under her feet.

She had passed the house, the equipment shed, and was almost to the barn when suddenly she went rigid with terror as a deep-chested roar shattered the stillness. Shadow — she had forgotten him! His racing footsteps drummed along the ground toward her and she called frantically, as loud as she dared. "Shadow! It's me!" Whether he heard her or scented her didn't matter. In a moment his big tongue was scrubbing her cheek and his tail was thumping her as he danced around with the delight of having unexpected company. Katty Lou fended him off with the bundle, making shushing noises and straining to hear any sound that might come from the house. Evidently the Marches were used to Shadow's night alarms. There was no sound and a moment later she was slipping through the big sliding door into the shelter of the barn.

At once she heard the metallic rattle of halter chains, the thump of heavy hoofs on the wooden floor, and a low, throaty nicker. She knew that heads had turned toward her and that curious eyes were seeking her out in the darkness. "Whoever you are," she called softly, "it's only me." Flicking on the light, she started along between the rows of stalls, recognizing the occupant of each as she passed. They were the ones who would be used for lessons in the morning. There were Tallulah, Baby, Lord Harry, Blister and Sam, and she spoke to each of them by name. Just as she had expected, Pepper was in the big box stall at the end. There, a tiny lump in a corner, was Tipsy, who raised his head from his bed of clean straw just long enough to give Katty Lou one sleepy look before he let it drop.

Leaving the bundle just outside the door, she went in, patted Pepper reassuringly and sat down beside the colt. Then she lifted his head, slid under it and laid it in her lap.

For a while she was content to lean back and stroke the soft little neck, pretending she had come here just for the fun of it and would be back to see him tomorrow, and the next day, and the next. Pepper's sudden stirring in the straw and the grunt she made as she lay down brought Katty Lou back to reality and she knew the rain was coming down much harder now. She could hear its steady beating on the vaulted roof high above, running from the gutters in a droning stream. Looking down at Tipsy, though she couldn't see him in the dark, she said softly, "I only came to say goodbye." Her own words threatened to bring the tears again, and she hurried on. "But I won't go so far I can't come back and see you some time." It was comforting to talk, and she even began to believe that what she was saying could actually happen. ". . . I'm going to find a house with real nice people in it and I'm going to work for them. I'm really very good at cooking and sewing and cleaning and — oh, all kinds of things. I'll be so useful that after a while they'll even begin to pay me a little money. That's when I can start coming to see you. On my day off — *that's* when I'll come. And every time I'll bring you something — carrots and things — because by that time you'll like them. . . ."

The more she talked the more possible it all seemed, until after a while it was as if it were already happening. It would be a neat little house with a nice old lady living in it who really needed a girl to work for her. Katty Lou would have a pretty room of her own with bright-colored cur-

tains at the windows and pictures of horses all
around the walls. And on Sundays the nice old
lady would hand her her week's wages — maybe
as much as five dollars — and say, "Now you run
along and see all your horse friends. Have a good
time — and I won't wait up for you. . . ."

It was Tipsy who woke her up, struggling to his
feet to demand his breakfast. She opened her eyes,
stared around in bewilderment. What place was
this? How did she — In an instant she had leaped
to her feet, slipped out of the stall and was snatch-
ing up her bundle. The rain had stopped and already sunlight was angling in through the partly
open door.

Poised to run to the door, she froze abruptly.
From the house had come the sound of a door
slammed carelessly, then the thud of high-heeled
boots on the porch, and voices — first Cal's, then
Homer's.

Her eyes darted wildly around. The Marches
mustn't find her! If they did they would take her
back. Perhaps they might not want to, but they
would feel they had to. She knew that. But where
could she hide? The voices were coming closer.

Then she caught sight of the ladder that led up to the hayloft. She climbed with awkward desperation, hampered at every step by the bulky bundle, and disappeared through the opening at the top just as she heard the rumble of the big door, which one of the men had slid farther open. Hurrying noiselessly over the carpet of straw, she crouched, trembling, between two towering piles of baled hay.

The voices reached her clearly as Homer and Cal went about the job of feeding the horses. They were arguing. "But it's too big an order!" Cal said protestingly. "We can't greenbreak eleven two-year-olds between now and the first of August — Hah! Blister, you old devil, get over! — Not and keep up with all the other work."

"But I keep telling you," Homer said, "there are the evenings! It doesn't get dark these nights — Gimme time, Baby, gimme *time* — until nearly ten, and —"

"Evenings, evenings, evenings!" Cal broke in. "Figure it out. Half an hour twice a day for eleven colts — eleven hours a day. You show me where eleven hours a day are going to come from."

"Among the three of us," Homer insisted, "we could do it. And for the bonus they're offering I think we —" He broke off, was silent a moment, then called, "Say, what's this doing here?"

"What's what doing where?"

"A flashlight," Homer said. "In Pepper's stall." Ten feet above his head Katty Lou's heart leaped into her throat.

"How should I know?" came Cal's careless voice. "Maybe the old mare's scared of the dark."

Homer's voice was thoughtful. "It wasn't there last night when I put her in."

"You figure it out, sonny," Cal said, his voice coming from farther away. "I've got to go down yonder and bring up a couple more nags." Katty Lou could hear his footsteps as he left the barn. After that there was silence broken only by the rhythmic crunching of oats and an occasional snort as a horse cleared the dust of the hay from his nose. There was no sound from Homer. If Katty Lou could have seen him her heart would have beat even faster. He was staring at the flashlight with a puzzled frown. Slowly then, his eyes moved down to his boots. Carefully he moved each foot

179

back and peered down at the place where they had been. In the dust were two perfect boot prints. And nearby were other prints, smaller ones that were not made by boots. Slowly his eye followed to the spot where the prints ended. Just as slowly, his head came up and he looked at the opening to the hayloft. Then he began to climb.

15

THE scrape of Homer's boots on the rungs of the ladder set Katty Lou to clawing at the wall of bales beside her, trying frantically to move a bale and make a hole big enough to burrow into.

She wasn't afraid of Homer; something deep inside her longed desperately for him to find her. But there was a deeper thing. It was the old fear that had ruled her so long. It wasn't a thing that could be thought about or reasoned about, it could only be acted upon, and the only way to act on it was to run or to hide.

Now she could do neither. The bales were immovable as stone and there was no place to run except straight into Homer's arms. So Katty Lou gave up and crouched there, listening, waiting.

Soon his feet were swishing through the litter of straw — nearer — and then he appeared, framed like a full-length portrait in the opening between the stacks of bales. There was a moment of tense silence while his eyes took in the fear written in hers and in every line of her huddled body. She didn't know that she reminded him of the first time he had seen her, crouched the same way in the thicket outside the barn. His eyes took in the bundle too.

He had looked troubled but now he smiled. "Hide and seek — at *my* age!" he said casually. "Now it's your turn to be 'it.'" He glanced at his watch. "Say, I haven't had my breakfast yet, and I'll bet you haven't either. Come on."

Katty Lou looked down at her lap. She could only shake her head, wordlessly. The fear was gone now and she felt only a bitter humiliation that he should have found her like this, cringing like a whipped puppy. Why — *why* did she act this way? It was only one more proof that she was different from other girls.

Homer didn't seem to notice she hadn't answered him. He reached down, his big hand closed over hers, and pulled her to her feet. "Let's go," he said. "It'll give me the chance I've been wanting — to tell you what that Tipsy did on Sunday. The little stinker!" Nodding toward the bundle, he said, "We'll get your stuff later," and started toward the ladder.

Katty Lou followed, because he was Homer, and because, after all, there was nothing else to do.

At the bottom he reached up, circling her waist with his hands, and swung her the rest of the way down. He started talking at once and kept it up as they walked side by side to the house. "Wait'll you hear. That little rascal darn near broke up the show — *did* break it up for a while, as a matter of fact. And how the audience loved it! Gee, I sure did wish you were there to see it. But then, if you'd been there it wouldn't have happened. . . ."

By the time he had opened the back door for her and pushed her gently ahead of him into the big cluttered kitchen, Katty Lou was so beside herself with curiosity about what Tipsy had done that there was room for little else in her mind. It was as if the last two desolate days had been wiped from the pages of time and this was a day unclouded by fear and guilt and heartache.

Old Evan was at the kitchen table finishing his coffee. He looked up, startled, as they came in.

Then his furrowed face broke into a grin. "Well, by all the dimes in Denver!" he began. "Look what we —" He broke off abruptly and scrubbed at his mouth with a napkin. Katty Lou couldn't know that, behind her, Homer had given his head a quick, violent shake, frowning fiercely, then jerked it toward the door behind him. Evan stood up quickly, scooped up his stained and battered hat from a chair, and headed for the door. "Well," he said, a little lamely, "off to the rodeo!"

Homer stepped to the stove and switched on a burner. "Want to go wash up while I whomp up a little chow?" he said over his shoulder. "Through the hall and turn right."

Still boiling with curiosity, Katty Lou went to the bathroom and washed her hands and face. While she dried them she could hear Homer rattling dishes, banging pans and whistling.

He kept her in suspense until they had sat down to plates of bacon and eggs and tall glasses of milk. If she hadn't been so confused, curious and excited she might have known by the stack of dirty dishes in the sink that the Marches — including Homer — had already eaten.

He grinned at her across the table. "All right now," he said, "you eat your breakfast while I tell you the story."

With the first obedient bite Katty Lou realized she was ravenous, but she could hardly take her eyes from Homer's face long enough to cut each bite.

"It was at the Sunday show," he began. "Biggest crowd of all. The ponies had made their entry, you know, just the way it was when you were there, and we were starting on the drill. I had the younger sister of the Saxton girl — the one who drives Trumpet, you know — I had her holding Tipsy.

"Well, we got to the thread-the-needle part where the two lines pass through each other at right angles." Katty Lou nodded eagerly. She could see it all as clearly as if she were watching it. "Right then," Homer went on, "that crazy Tipsy made up his mind he'd had just about enough of this monkey-business. He was going to get to his mama — or *else*. And the little girl holding him was goofing off, watching the show instead of tending to business, and not holding tight to his rope." He took a large bite of bacon and chewed deliberately. There was a mischievous light in his eyes.

Katty Lou swallowed her own bite too hurriedly and nearly choked on it. "What — what did he do?" she asked. She didn't realize those were the first words she had spoken since she was talking to Tipsy himself the night before. The look of satisfaction on Homer's face escaped her.

"Do?" he said. "What *didn't* he do? He broke loose and made a dash for the middle of things, tripping over his rope and yelling for mama every step of the way. First thing he did was run right smack in front of Tiny. Tiny tried to stop and when he couldn't do that he swerved, nearly tipping his cart over. He slowed just enough so that Baldy, the next in line, darn near ran over Tiny's cart, so Baldy swerved the *other* way. And so it went, all down the line. Meanwhile Tipsy got mixed up and lost sight of Pepper, who was close to getting out of hand herself, because of all the racket he was making. He went tearing around through all those ponies and carts until we had the doggonedest mix-up you ever saw — everything in a tangle — wheels of one cart locked with another — kids yelling at their ponies — and at me — and the crowd going crazy.

"And *then* you know what the little devil did?"

"*What?*" The word came out like a cork from a bottle.

"He located Pepper at last — and he walked up to her as calm as you please —" Homer paused dramatically. "And he helped himself to a bit of lunch!"

"Oh-h-h-h!" cried Katty Lou ecstatically and Homer laughed.

"Oh-h-h is right," he said. "That's exactly what the audience said — the biggest, thunderingest, longest-drawn-out Oh-h-h I ever heard in my life — and then they all jumped out of their seats and cheered and clapped and stamped and whistled like crazy. I don't know how long they kept it up. I was too busy out there unscrambling that mess. I'll bet that arena hasn't heard anything like it since the day it was built. I thought the roof was going to come off."

"And *then* what happened?" Katty Lou wished fervently that the story could go on forever.

"Well, we took those ponies out, lined 'em up, and started all over again. And you can bet that little girl kept a tight grip on Tipsy's rope that time. Everything went like clockwork and we got a whale of a hand when it was over."

He tipped his chair back, clasping his hands behind his head, and smiled at her. "So that's the story of your bad-acting pony colt." Katty Lou smiled back at him, picturing the wild confusion caused by one small, willful animal.

Then her smile winked out like a candle in the wind because Homer said, "And now we come to another story — about Katty Lou."

She tried to pretend she couldn't imagine what he was talking about, but it was no use. She waited for him to go on.

"You know," he said, looking up at the ceiling, "the most natural thing in the world to do when the going gets rough is to run away. We all do it — people and animals too. As a matter of fact, it's the only sensible thing to do sometimes. Take horses. Running away is the only weapon they have. The only thing they can do to keep alive. Well, it would be the same with people too — except for one thing. You can't run away from something that's inside you, and that's exactly where most of the things are that people want to run from — inside them. Okay. So what do they do? They do one of two things: They go on running and they never stop, and if that happens they're never happy as long as they live. Or, they stop running and they look around at whatever's after them, and they say, 'You don't seem so doggone scary in the light of day.' And they dare it to come on and do its worst. *That's* when they find out they've won the fight before it even started." He looked at her and said softly, "Katty Lou, which way is it going to be with you?"

Katty Lou stared down at her hands. They were squeezing the table edge so tight they hurt. "I —" she began, but something clicked in her throat and she had to begin again, in a voice that was little more than a whisper. "I — I'm not going to run away any more."

"That's my girl!" said Homer triumphantly. "What *are* you going to do?"

"I'm going to —" Katty Lou hesitated. If she said what was in her mind, then she'd have to do it, and it was an impossible thing to do. If she didn't say it, then . . . With a reckless, dizzy feeling, like diving off a high board for the first time, she raised her head and looked straight at Homer.

"I'm going to go back," she said, and with every word her voice grew stronger. "And I'm going to — to tell them I'm sorry I ran away, and that I won't ever do it again, and I won't — I won't —" She stumbled over the next part, because it was the hardest of all to say. "And I won't come over here any more!"

The whole house seemed to shake as Homer lunged to his feet. In one step he was by her side, his big hands reaching down to her. In the next instant she felt herself plucked out of her chair and hoisted aloft to the length of his arms. With her head only an inch or so from the ceiling, she looked down, gasping, into a big face that was nothing but grin, and heard the joyful boom of his voice. "Yee--ow! You did it!" Then he set her down as softly as if she had been a paper doll. Still grinning, he added, "Anyway, you *said* it, and that's two thirds of the battle." He put his hands on her shoulders again and turned her around to face the kitchen door. "Okay. Get going."

"N-now?" Katty Lou said, a horrible sinking feeling in her stomach.

"Now," said Homer firmly. She felt his hand in the middle of her back, gently pushing her toward

the door. "And don't worry," he added. "You'll be
seeing me again, sooner than you think."

She went out the door and around the house
and down the lane on legs that belonged to some-
body else. The lane seemed to stretch on forever.
Little pools of rainwater glistened in the ruts as
she walked along the loose gravel in the middle. It
seemed a lifetime ago that she had walked up it in
the rainy darkness. Not once did she look back.
She didn't need to. She knew that Homer's eyes
were on her every step of the long way. It was almost as though his hand were still on her back,
pushing her forward.

Long though the March lane seemed, she found
herself, all too soon, crossing the smooth black-top
of the road, turning in through the gap in the
Kirby's laurel hedge, trudging, with as much effort
as if she were walking in mud, toward the house.
Her throat was dry and her heart beat wildly, but
there was something in her of the crazy, larger-
than-life feeling that had come over her as she
marched around the arena in Salem. A shrill little
voice inside her kept shouting over and over and
over, "I'm doing it, I'm doing it, I'm doing it!"

Then the front door burst open and there stood

Mrs. Kirby, shorter and squarer than ever in her robe and slippers, a look of amazement on her face. The words came pouring out of her in a torrent. "My goodness gracious sakes, child, where have you been? We've been nearly out of our minds!" Without waiting for an answer, she whirled and called, "Arthur, she's here! She's come back!"

In a moment Mr. Kirby appeared in the doorway beside her, looking kindly and relieved. The flood of Mrs. Kirby's words went on, but Katty Lou heard Mr. Kirby say, "Well!" and then again, "Well!"

Katty Lou climbed the three front steps, taking a deep breath on each, and on the porch she stopped, waiting for Mrs. Kirby to run out of breath. When she did, Katty Lou said, "I ran away." She was amazed how easily the words came out, and knew it was that way because she had already said them to Homer. "I ran away," she repeated. "I wasn't going to come back, but I did, because — well, because it's wrong to run away, and Homer said —"

"Homer!" Mrs. Kirby said. "Then you've been —?"

"Never mind all that right now," Mr. Kirby put in with unaccustomed forcefulness. "Main thing is you've come back. Let's go in and have a little breakfast."

Katty Lou followed them into the kitchen, frantic over the interruption. She hadn't finished what she had to say, and at any moment her courage might desert her. When they turned, she looked at first one and then the other and said, a little desperately, "I won't run away any more, and I won't — go over to the Marches'."

For once, Mrs. Kirby seemed at a loss for words. She sat down distractedly at the breakfast table. Mr. Kirby stood, looking down at Katty Lou with a strange expression. Mrs. Kirby's hands came down on the table with a soft thump. "I don't know," she said. "I just don't know what to say. Maybe you'll keep your promise and maybe you won't. I've even been thinking that — that maybe you'd be better off in some other home."

She paused and Katty Lou thought with dismay of being sent somewhere else and never seeing Tipsy again, even from a distance.

Mrs. Kirby went on. "And then I thought — Oh dear, I just don't know *what* to think, but Miss

O'Connor should be here any minute now, and she — Oh, my goodness!" Her hands flew to her uncombed hair. "I can't greet her like this!" She hurried into the bedroom.

Mr. Kirby, searching Katty Lou's troubled face, leaned down suddenly, and gave her shoulder an awkward pat. "Don't worry, now," he said. "Nothing's been decided yet." He hesitated, then added, "You're a brave one, girl." He turned and began to take breakfast dishes from a cupboard. Katty Lou jumped to help him, glad to have something to do. A few minutes later car wheels crunched on the gravel outside and they both looked out to see the county car come to a halt in the driveway. "Run let her in, will you, girl?" Mr. Kirby said.

Miss O'Connor was closing the car door when Katty Lou pounded down the porch steps and across the lawn. Miss O'Connor looked startled, unbelieving, then she smiled radiantly, took hold of Katty Lou's shoulders and squeezed. "For heaven's sake!" she said. "Here I thought you were halfway to California or someplace, and instead —"

"I ran away!" Katty Lou interrupted, the words coming out in a rush. "But I came back. I came back all by myself — that is — I *came* by myself, but it was Homer that —"

Miss O'Connor looked puzzled. "Homer?"

"Homer March," Katty Lou hurried on. "He found me in the hayloft, and he told me why it was bad to run away, and so —"

"Now wait, honey!" Miss O'Connor was smiling again but she looked serious all the same. "I think we'd better go in and settle down and start from the beginning."

When Mrs. Kirby came out of the bedroom, combed and dressed, she came talking. She told Miss O'Connor, in detail and with a few side excursions, everything that had happened from the time she saw the photograph in the paper to the moment Katty Lou had appeared on the front walk. Miss O'Connor listened politely and when Mrs. Kirby stopped at last she turned to Katty Lou, who sat at the table with the others, the glass of milk Mr. Kirby had poured for her standing untasted. "Now, honey," she said, "I guess nobody but you can tell us the rest of it."

At first it was like swimming in cold soup. Every sentence, every word, took tremendous effort, and she didn't dare take her eyes from the sugar bowl. But soon she found the words coming more easily, still more easily, and as the story neared its end she found she could steal a glance now and then at the silent listeners. She left out nothing but her plan to get a job with a kind old lady. Now, even so short a time later, the plan seemed like something she might have thought up at the age of six. Her hiding in the hayloft seemed childish too, but she told about it anyway.

She was in the middle of the part about Homer and what he had said to her at the breakfast table when Mrs. Kirby, who was facing the front window, gave a little gasp. "What in the world —?" she said.

As Katty Lou and the others looked out the window, she gasped too.

Angling across the road from the March lane to the Kirby front walk came the March men — all three of them. They wore clean shirts and their boots were freshly shined. Katty Lou felt excitement surging up in her — and uneasiness too.

Mrs. Kirby said, "Why — why, they're coming *here!* The nerve!"

"Oh, now Martha," Mr. Kirby said. "They're not as bad as all that."

"I'm not so sure, Mr. Kirby." Miss O'Connor sounded grim.

The clatter of three pairs of boots on the porch brought Mr. and Mrs. Kirby to their feet. "Arthur, I don't want to talk to them!" Mrs. Kirby said.

"We can't turn them away from the door, Martha. After all, they're our neighbors. And just talking can't hurt anything." He started toward the door and she stood looking after him, clasping and unclasping her hands.

There was a rumble of greetings out of which Homer's voice came clear. ". . . want to apologize, Mr. Kirby, for barging in like this, but we feel as if we've got a stake in what happens to Katty Lou."

Then Evan's voice. "Homer's purely gone on that young'un. Matter of fact, we all are."

"Guess that gives us something in common," Mr. Kirby said. He cleared his throat nervously. "Well, everybody's out in the kitchen. Maybe you'd have a cup of coffee with us."

The three big men came in, their white hats in their hands, and the room seemed too small for them. Homer said, "Good morning, Mrs. Kirby.

We want to apologize to you too for intruding like this, but —"

"Quite all right," said Mrs. Kirby in a tone that plainly showed it was not all right.

Homer started to say something else, then closed his mouth. He had seen Miss O'Connor for the first time. His face lighted in a smile. "I'll be darned — Eileen O'Connor! I didn't know *you* were the Miss O'Connor I've been hearing about."

"How do you do — Homer," Miss O'Connor said stiffly.

Why? Katty Lou thought frantically. *Why* doesn't she like him?

His smile vanished and his face was expressionless. "This is my brother Cal," he said. "And my father, Evan March."

A puzzled frown appeared on Miss O'Connor's face. "I don't understand," she said. "The Evan March I met was — well — quite different."

"Never heard of another Evan March," the old man said. "Where'd you meet him, miss?"

"Right in front of your — that is, *his* — barn. Just across the road."

Evan screwed up his craggy face, completely

baffled. "That beats all. Anyways, anybody that said he was me was a plain out liar."

"Wait a minute!" Homer spoke abruptly. He turned to Miss O'Connor. "May I ask why you were over there?"

Miss O'Connor blushed but looked him straight in the eye. "I went to find out for myself what sort of people Katty Lou was associating with."

"And you found out?"

"Yes," she said icily, "I did."

"From this person who said he was Evan March?"

"Of course."

Homer's smile was a little grim as he said to his father, "Now I begin to see the reason for our chilly reception here." He turned back to Miss O'Connor. "Was this man you talked to shoeing a horse?"

Her answer went unheard because Cal and Evan burst out explosively at the same instant. "Orvie!"

"Eileen," Homer said, "the man you talked to is the best blacksmith in the county, and the biggest liar in the world. I don't know what he told you, and I'd rather not hear, but I can guarantee this: Whatever he told you, there wasn't a word of truth in it."

Miss O'Connor looked uncomfortable but not convinced. "But," she said hesitantly, "he *couldn't* have been lying. It was all in such" — she shuddered slightly — "such *detail*."

"You don't have to take my word for it," Homer said. "Ask Katty Lou."

Forgetting the size of her audience in her eagerness to help clear up this awful misunderstanding, Katty Lou didn't wait to be asked. "Oh, Miss O'Connor," she burst out, "he *is* a terrible liar! I heard him once, and I almost believed what he was saying, even when I knew all the time it wasn't true!"

Miss O'Connor looked at Cal with troubled, bewildered eyes. "Then — then there never *was* any murder charge against you in California, and —"

Cal whistled sharply through his teeth and then grinned. "Looks like Orvie really gave us the full treatment. No, Miss O'Connor, I've got my bad habits, but killing people isn't one of them."

"And you —" She was looking at Homer now. "You weren't court-martialed and thrown out of the Marine Corps for —" She shook her head as though to clear away her last stubborn doubts. "Of course you weren't. I don't know why I —"

"Orvie's life is pretty dull," Homer said. "He livens it up with the help of his imagination."

Miss O'Connor smiled ruefully. "I guess I owe you all an apology," she said. Then, to Katty Lou, "Oh, honey, I *did* make a mess of things! I should have known better, should have checked into —"

"Now don't go to frettin' yerself, miss," Evan said. "*Everybody* swallows Orvie's yarns till they get to know him. Took me a good six months to catch onto him."

"Well," said Homer. "I'm glad we've got *that* straightened out." He turned to Mrs. Kirby, who had sat down across from Miss O'Connor, silent probably for one of the longest times in her life. "Now we can get on to the reason, or one of them, why we came horning in over here, Mrs. Kirby. We thought that if we could get a little better acquainted, you wouldn't — that is —"

He floundered to a standstill and Cal came to his rescue. "We're goodwill ambassadors, you might say — for ourselves."

Caught between her prejudices and her impulse to be polite, Mrs. Kirby floundered too. "I'm sure

I have nothing against — er — getting better acquainted. I —"

"Mrs. Kirby!" Evan interrupted, his grizzled eyebrows fairly bristling with earnestness and some inner excitement. "We want to *prove* we got this little gal's best interests at heart. Miss O'Connor, we talked it over — me and Cal and Homer. We decided —"

"Dad!" cut in Homer, but the old man raised his voice. "Miss O'Connor, we want to *adopt* her!"

There was a moment of silence in which Katty Lou felt as though the breath had been knocked out of her. Then the others all began talking at once. It was most confusing and she couldn't sort out much of it except that Mrs. Kirby was saying, "Well, I *never!*" Cal, in low, urgent tones, was telling Evan to be quiet and let Homer do the talking. And Miss O'Connor, speaking rapidly, was saying something about the law, and about men having to be married before they could adopt anybody. She understood all too clearly, though, when Miss O'Connor turned to her with a strained sort of smile. "Run outside and play a while, will you, honey? We'll have a talk later on."

Katty Lou was just closing the front door behind her when the voice of Evan was raised again. "Gol-durn it then, boy, you'll have to *get* married. I been tellin' you fer years . . ."

The next half hour or so was endless for Katty Lou. She paced nervously around the yard, trying, without any real hope, to think of something to do. At last she gave up and sat on the grass with her back against the big old cherry tree in the front yard. She could think of nothing but whether she could get up the nerve to tell Homer about the wonderful, glowing, too-much-to-be-hoped-for idea that had sprung into her mind the instant she had closed the front door behind her. She was just deciding that she *had* to tell him, nerve or no nerve, when she heard the scraping of chairs on the kitchen floor and the thump of footsteps. She jumped to her feet and began swinging from a branch of the tree, trying to look as if she had been doing it for some time. Her heart was pounding.

The door opened and out came Miss O'Connor. Katty Lou's glance flew to her face, and her racing heartbeat threatened to choke her, for Miss O'Connor wore a smile so radiant it could mean only one thing — good news. She hurried down the steps and across the grass. "Everything's love-

ly," she said in her bubbliest voice. "Mrs. Kirby
has changed her mind. You may go to see your
pony any time you like!"

First Katty Lou wanted to laugh, and then she
wanted to cry, so she did neither. She merely stood
quite still and stared up at Miss O'Connor with
dark and glowing eyes.

Then Homer came out, smiling down at her.
"Well, nymph," he said, "it looks like, between us,
we've done a good day's work."

Then Evan's voice, from the porch. "Remember
now, ma'am, any time you want ridin' lessons —
free, gratis, and fer nothin' — you just give me the
word."

Mrs. Kirby's answer was a peal of laughter, almost girlish. "Me, on a horse," she said. "Now that
would be a sight!"

"You got the hands for it, ma'am," Evan said.
"I can tell good hands when I see 'em. Well, we'll
be seein' you folks!" He and Cal started toward
the road. As Cal strode past Katty Lou, his right
eye closed in a long, slow wink, and he tipped his
head significantly toward Homer and Miss O'Connor.

It was probably the wink that gave Katty Lou

the courage to do what she had been bursting to do all during her endless wait in the yard. Anyway, she knew that if she didn't do it now, this very instant, she would never again have the courage. She reached up and pulled insistently at Homer's sleeve until, understanding, he bent down so that her lips could reach his ear. "You could —" she began in a whisper. Her throat went dry and she had to make a new start. "You could — marry *her!*"

She knew, though she didn't dare look at him, that it was a long moment before he straightened up again, very slowly. She didn't dare look at Miss O'Connor either but she could hear the smile in her voice when she said, "So you have secrets, you two? Well, let's go. I've been invited to go over and meet your friend Tipsy."

Katty Lou looked up then and saw that Homer was giving a great deal of attention to setting his hat on his head. She could see too that he was vastly relieved that Miss O'Connor had brought up another subject. "I thought you'd like to perform the introduction, nymph," he said, "and maybe show Miss O'Connor around the place."

After that, in a kind of daze — like a good dream that went on long after most good dreams would have ended in everyday wakefulness — she walked with the two of them across the road, up the lane and into the barn where Tipsy and Pepper waited. She saw Miss O'Connor drop to her knees beside Tipsy and hug him, saying, "Oh, Katty Lou, I can *see* why you couldn't stay away!" She showed Miss O'Connor the thicket in which she had spent so many happy hours, the red and white carts she had helped to paint, the harness she had saddle-soaped — all the evidences of the thousand-and-one things she had done with Homer in the happy weeks that lay behind, the happy weeks that no longer had to come to an end. She wasn't even aware that she was talking as she had never talked before and that now and then the two people she loved most in all the world exchanged glances that showed how much her happiness meant to them.

She was riding Pepper out in the pony drill area to show Miss O'Connor how much she had learned — and to tell the truth, she was showing off a little, the way nearly all little girls sometimes do — when she stole a quick glance at her audience and realized she didn't have an audience at all.

They were sitting on a bench near the side of the house, under the big English walnut tree.

They weren't paying any attention to her and Pepper. They were looking at each other, Homer's head bent down toward Miss O'Connor's, and they were laughing at something one of them had said.

For just one moment Katty Lou felt a little hurt, a little left out. The next moment she slid off Pepper's back and led her cautiously, almost on tiptoe, to where Tipsy was tied at the corner of the barn. Just as cautiously, she led them both through the big barn door to the box stall where she had spent the night a whole lifetime ago.

Closing the lower door of the stall behind her, she kneeled and wrapped both arms around Tipsy's sturdy little shoulders. Very softly, she said, "I'm going to cross my fingers. You can't do that, but you could cross your legs. You've got four of them — and it might help."

She was thinking, wishing, hoping — even though she knew she had no right to hope — that maybe, just *maybe*, please God, she might after all get to have a mother and father of her very own.

EPILOGUE

THE scents of hay and horses and dry July heat made an intoxicating blend. The stands overhead rumbled with the tread of feet and the hum of hundreds of voices.

Katty Lou March, in her crisp white blouse, a red silk scarf knotted at the side of her throat and a white one corralling her ebony hair in a pony-tail, drank in the fragrance and reveled in the sounds as her fingers moved swiftly and surely, plaiting the last of the red and white ribbons into Pepper's mane.

Behind her, in the same stall, Tipsy munched lazily at the hay before him. Red and white rib-bons were braided into his mane too, and it was much more than a mere wisp of a mane now. His coat was brushed to a satiny gloss, like Pepper's, though he wasn't even to appear in the show. Nearly as tall as Pepper, though slimmer, he was still convinced that a mother is a colt's best friend.

"Katty Lou!" She looked up and smiled as a girl of about eleven with curly brown hair poked her head into the stall behind Pepper. She too was wearing the March colors. "Katty Lou, would you come help me when you're done? I just can't get that bad ol' Trumpet to hold still while I brush his tail!"

"Okay, Sue," she said. "I'll be through here in a second."

A minute or two later she was brushing Trumpet's flowing tail while she held his rump pinned to the side of the stall with one cocked hip. Suddenly she stopped, a prickle of excitement running up her back. From the never-never land where amplifiers are always hidden came a sharp crackling sound, and then the voice of the announcer: "Welcome, ladies and gentlemen, to the twelfth annual Salem Horse Show! May I remind you that there will be another performance this evening at eight, and a third . . ."

A pair of shiny boots and a pair of long legs came into view, clad in tight Western pants with red piping at the seams. Katty Lou looked up quickly into the smiling eyes of Homer March.

"Better harness up, nymph," he said. "We're fourth on the program this time."

She straightened, dropped Trumpet's tail and dusted her hands together. "All right, Dad," she said, then looked at him with a sideways smile. "Gee," she said, "I've got butterflies."

He laughed. "Think what you'll have next year when you'll be driving that Tipsy horse. He'll be jumpy as a cat in a kennel. Go on, now, get your pony!" Still smiling, he watched as she hurried off, then moved on to the next stall and looked in. "Snap it up, Bobby. We haven't much time. And when you get out there remember what I've been saying all summer long. Keep your distance on those turns! Don't crowd!"

Standing at Pepper's head, Katty Lou looked back along the line of ponies and carts as they waited their cue to move to the gate. She felt the butterflies still fluttering, but she felt a sort of swelling too — of pride, of all sorts of things she couldn't put a name to. After that came an urge she couldn't deny. She called breathlessly to the driver behind her, "Back in a second!" and dashed to the stall.

Tipsy wasn't calm now. He had turned around

as far as his chain and the corner of the stall would let him, trying to see where Pepper had gone. With one dainty white forefoot he pawed nervously, scattering his hay around. Katty Lou bent and hugged him quickly. Then she put her face close to his head and said, "One kiss, Tipsy — just for luck?"

He looked a little sulky for a moment, but then he raised his head and nuzzled her cheek with his velvety lips. A laugh bubbled out of her because she could tell he had his mind on other things. Then she ran quickly back, the ponytail bouncing with every step, jumped into her cart and took the reins in hand.

Homer was standing by Pepper now, giving every cart a last keen look. "Still have butterflies?" he asked, looking down at her.

She nodded emphatically. "But I'm not really scared. Oh — where's Miss O'Con —" She interrupted herself, laughing. "Darn it, I *must* be excited — Where's *Mother* sitting? I want to be sure and see her."

"You'll see her all right. She's in the very seat you had last year."

"Does she — does she feel all right?"

"Feel all right?" he echoed, looking puzzled. Then he laughed and gave her shoulder a squeeze. "Of course she does, worry-wart! I keep telling you — Christmastime is a long way off."

To herself Katty Lou agreed that it was the longest way off a Christmastime had ever been. It was almost unbearable to have to wait that long to find out which she was going to have — a little brother or a little sister to take care of.

1907   F.W.